The Even
T.A. Moore

Ex Libris

Published by Morrígan Books
Östra Promenaden 43
602 29 Norrköping, Sweden
www.Morríganbooks.com

Editors: Mark S. Deniz

ISBN 978-91-977605-4-6

Cover and internal art by Stephanie Mui-Pun Law ©2008
Cover art design by Reece Notley ©2008

First Published September 2008
The Even © T.A. Moore

The moral rights of the authors have been asserted.

All characters in this publication, other than those clearly in the public domain, are fictitious and any resemblance to real persons, living or dead, is purely coincidental.

All rights reserved. No part of this publication may be reproduced or transmitted in any forms by any means, electronic or mechanical including photocopying, recording or any information retrieval system, without prior permission, in writing, from the publisher.

This book is sold subject to the condition that it shall not, by way of trade or otherwise, be lent, resold, hired out, or otherwise circulated without the publisher's prior consent in any form of binding or cover other than that in which it is published and without a similar condition including this condition being imposed on the subsequent purchaser.

Printed and bound in England by Biddles
www.biddles.co.uk

*To my Mum and Grandparents:
You were right, I could do it.*

*With thanks to
The Arts Council of Northern Ireland for their support.*

Foreword

Elaine Cunningham

Immortality is never absolute. Gods die in glorious battle, or fall to a greater god's curse, or simply fade from memory. Some of them, in a pragmatic concession to the whims of mortal worshipers, trade their deity for sainthood. But pilgrimage is a fashion too arduous to long endure; the relics made from the bones of virgin nuns crumble into dust, and in time saints, too, are forgotten.

Immortality is never without price. One of the heaviest of these is ennui. After a few centuries, even the greatest pleasures pale. In an effort to stave off madness, immortal beings seek new forms of distraction: games of chance, political treachery, or, as Lenith the Faceless observes, a virtue whose attainment lies beyond one's grasp.

Not that most gods are concerned with virtue.

More often, immortals find cruel amusement in toying with those less powerful: mortals, the fey, even their own offspring — mongrels begat upon the Daughters of Eve. So it is in the Even, a land that lies outside of Time, a place where discarded legends hawk their wares in the marketplace and forgotten gods live in squalor.

One of these is Lenith, formerly an Etruscan goddess and a guardian of the gate to the Deathlands. Now she's a gambler with a crushing debt and a spirit equally weighted down by cynicism. The only things she holds sacred are her own independence and the immutable laws of a deal. When she's offered a particularly intriguing deal-along with a chance to retire her debt-she accepts, reasoning that it is impossible to cheat Death and win.

But "winning" may not be what the mad gods desire.

In this grim fable, the stakes are suicide by Apocalypse, and the question is what can endure, and what refuses to end.

One

The young Yekumi stood at the top of the Stairway of a Thousand Steps. He had been stripped of the marks and signs of his rank. The cloth of gold had been torn from his clothes, the gems pried from his ivory skin and the great feathers had been plucked from his wings. All they left him was the glory of his caste, the shining gold hair and flawless skin, and the beauty of his fear.

He raised his hands to the crowds and yelled his last words defiantly. Also pointlessly, since the winds stole the words away before they could reach the assembled citizens. Finished, he dropped his arms to his side and looked at the upturned faces. Perhaps he thought they would intervene.

When the guards came for him he tried to take flight, swooping drunkenly over the courtyard while his mutilated wings rained blood on the crowd. Women held up their children over the crowd hoping to receive the benediction of Yekumi blood on their faces.

The Yekumi stayed aloft longer than expected, but his ruined wings could not bear him skywards. He crashed down onto the raddled, crooked stones that surrounded the Even. The crowd caught their breath and felt the world shift. Stone cracked and the gnomes pushed themselves, wet and muddy, from the earth's womb. Clots of dirt dribbled from their open jaws and their clawed fingers scraped the ground. Blinded by the daylight, they snorted and snuffled the air to find their prey.

For the first time in his life the Yekumi's white body was scuffed with dirt, his elbows and shins skinned. He scrambled to his knees and held out a pleading hand to the crowd. They drew back as one, fearful of looking sympathetic, and pulled skirts and cloaks close to their legs. The Yekumi's beautiful face twisted.

"Curse you," he spat. "May you –"

Then the gnomes were on him. They caught at his legs, claws tearing bloody rents in his skin and crawled over him. His screams were muffled by long, dirty fingers poked into his mouth. With their prey captured they returned to the earth that had borne them, dragging the thrashing Yekumi with them. His hands caught at the broken cobbles, tearing his nails and leaving bloody prints on the stone. Then he was gone. The earth shrugged closed behind the gnomes, leaving only the rippled, broken cobbles as evidence of their passing.

There was a quiet, almost reverent, silence. Then the first cry of the count rose from the crowd.

"Six marks." An old woman, wrapped in so many layers of clothes that she was round as an egg, made that claim. It was disputed by others who called the count at three or five or even nine, backing their claims with evidence of shadows and time-pieces and counted breaths.

The tallymen conferred; their heads together, and came to a consensus. They returned to their stalls while their spokesman, a sucker-fingered demon, clambered up the pedestal at the bottom of the stairs. He pulled a length of yellow cloth from his pants, bells sewn to the end, and waved it for silence. The bells rang out with a dull, brassy sound.

"Five marks," the demon croaked. "The count stands at five marks."

Lenith sighed ruefully. She'd caught herself a bloody feather but lost twenty stater. The treacher hadn't seemed to have it in him to last so long. Ah well. It was not the first time she had lost, nor the greatest amount.

She turned on her heel to leave and nearly tripped over a skinny child, sex impossible to determine under layers of dirt and rags, who shoved a leaflet into her hand.

"...presterjohninvitesyoutoameetingofthefifthmenwherehewill tellofthejoysoftheworldtocome", the child ra-ttled his spiel off without taking a breath.

"...onlytwocopperstatertojointhefifthmenandsave–"

He looked up into Lenith's face, and stuttered to silence. His

The Even

eyes skittered from side to side, looking for somewhere familiar to focus. They found nothing within the frame of thick, clay-white dreads that framed Lenith's pale, blank face. Only a plane of smooth, pink skin that ran from her broad brow to the curve of her chin. No eyes, although she seemed to see, no mouth although she could speak.

Braver men than this child had been shocked to silence by the sight. Even in the Even, where there were stranger things by far.

Lenith looked down at the leaflet he'd given her.

An exaggerated drawing of a woman, her clothing disarranged to show her flesh, leered over the legend 'The Whore of Even'. Beneath that the Fifth Men's evangelical polemic was laid out in smudgy ink-block print on cheap, pulp paper. God and Jesus and the End of the World; nothing new there then.

Lenith crouched down, putting herself at the same level as the boy. It did not serve to make him any more comfortable. He fidgeted in place and dropped his gaze to the small black buttons on her shirt.

"There's better ways to earn money than by preaching, boy," Lenith said. "Learn thieving, at least it's an honest trade."

The boy shrugged and gave her a sidelong scowl.

"Ain't no law against handing stuff out," he said.

"There's no law against spitting into the wind either," Lenith said, standing up. She crumpled the leaflet up in her hand. "That doesn't mean you should do it."

The boy looked up and away again quickly. He shrugged again. Lenith sighed and sent him on his way. She tossed the crumpled leaflet to the ground. It was trampled into the mud soon enough, joining the rest of the litter.

There were other urchins working the crowd. They ducked through legs and wriggled through gaps in the crowd, pressing their leaflets into reluctant hands and rattling off their Fifth Men litany. Most people ignored them or, as Lenith had, sent them on their way with a cuff around the ear for their temerity. A few, expansive after the entertainment and with fat pouches, tossed coppers. None of those coins would make it into the Fifth Men's coffers, but they weren't meant to. The leafleteers were allowed to keep the coins in return for passing out leaflets, it made them more enthusiastic.

One child, taller than the rest and cocky, tried to push past a Redcap and knocked his dyed cap askew with his elbow. Fresh gore dribbled down the Redcap's furrowed brow and dripped from the end of his nose. He snarled and knocked the boy to the ground with a casual backhand. The boy hit the pebbles, leaflets flying from his hands, and spat a curse at the Redcap. He underestimated the brutal fey's speed. It was on him before he could get to his feet again. A jagged knife pressed against his throat.

Before things could get out of hand Prester John himself was there. There was mud on the hem of his plain wool robes and the jewels had long since been pried from his crown; gone to fund the Fifth Men's pamphlets and meetings and books. He still had an air of authority though. That was not something that could be taken away; it was worked into the essence of him. He soothed the Redcap, an impressive feat considering that clan's fondness for bloodshed and slaughter, and got the child back on his feet. Within moments the child had gotten back to work and the Redcap was politely looking at a leaflet. He tossed it to the ground when Prester John left. For all Prester John's personal charisma, he couldn't convince the Even that his Fifth Men were anything but fools. Most of the crowd was more interested in knocking bloody chips of stone from the cobbles for souvenirs.

Lenith turned the feather between her fingers. There was still blood on the end and splattered over the feathers. Enbilulu was running a bait at the docks tonight, a Bishop-Fish against his Kelpie. The odds were running against the Fish. An upset could fatten Lenith's purse. She tucked the feather into her shirt, the barbs tickling her breast; perhaps it would bring her luck.

She left the Fifth Men to their proselytizing and headed into the city.

Two

Legend has this to say about the curse that lies on the Yekumi.

Twenty generations ago a Daughter of Lillith stood beneath the Even and cursed the blood and seed, the breath and bone, the flesh and thought of the Ruling House of Yekum with death in life. She invoked the spirits of the Earth to witness her curse, smiled darkly, or so the legend says, and took herself away to the lands beyond the city: unexplored, unmapped. She never returned.

A charged silence hung in the air in her wake. On the steps of the Palace the Yekumi waited with baited breath.

Nothing happened.

Eventually one of the younger kin laughed and walked out into the square to mock the vanished Daughter. His foot touched the earth. The stones of the square cracked, leaking sulphur and gouts of flame, and darkling gnomes clawed their way into the light. When they left they took the Yekumi youth with them. At night during the Dwindling Months his screams can still be heard, echoing up from some great hall under the earth.

None of the Yekumi has set foot to earth ever since, at least not willingly. In the Even Palace the basement and ground levels belong to the servants and lesser nobility. The higher the rank, the higher they lived. The Yekumi lived on the uppermost levels, where clouds drifted past the windows on stormy days; below only God himself. They rarely ventured far from the Palace. When they did go into the City proper they travelled on curtained litters, borne on the shoulders of servants.

Occasionally, when Yekum, Father of the Yekumi, felt of a particularly enquiring or wicked turn of mind, he tested the power of the curse.

Three

The bait was a disappointment. Lenith leant on the balcony, her shoulders jostling for space between a goat-headed creature and a human who clutched his ticket in sweating hands. She let her hands dangle and watched the Kelpie tear chunks from the Bishop-fish's black flanks. The Bishop-fish didn't even fight back. It just floundered and flapped, naked pate bobbing and slack mouth burping mangled Latin.

Blood turned the water pink.

At last, the Bishop-fish turned its cow-eyes skyward and sank under the water. The Kelpie frisked, shaking foam from its mane, and then dived down after it to finish it off. It would eat well tonight.

"Shit," Lenith sighed. She should have known better. Luck had never been within her dominion. That was the point, the lure. She tore her ticket in half and threw it away. The salty breeze caught the pieces and tossed them in the air before finally depositing them into the choppy waters below. A rain of other tickets fluttered down to join it. There was always someone in the Even willing to take a risk on long odds.

Below, standing on the short pier, Enbilulu clapped webbed hands together and smirked. He'd obviously made a profit off the fight. But then, he usually did.

Lenith pushed herself off the railing and shoved through the crowd, heading for the rickety stairs that led down from the gallery. She could feel it sway under her with each step. One of these days the whole edifice was going to collapse into the water and the Kelpie would eat well again. She stepped over a twitching tail-tip, kicking out when it caught at her ankle, and ducked beneath a dog-headed Kludde's wings.

The Even

The fey was waiting for her at the top of the stairs, crouched and spindly. No-one crowded it. The reek from the filthy rags that draped its stick-skinny frame kept them back. It grinned up at her, white teeth splitting the sharp, brown triangle of its face.

"Lost again, Faceless," it said. "You must be well out of pocket now. Empty of pocket, even."

"My business, and none of yours, Thistle," Lenith said. She stepped forwards. It didn't move, just twisting its head back at an awkward angle to look up at her. "Move aside."

The fey pouted. "Don't be so cruel, Faceless," it said. "It was an innocent question."

"There's nothing about you that's innocent, Thistle," Lenith said.

It moved suddenly, rising to its feet and pressing close to her side. The smell of it soured the air around her. It ran furred, nail-less fingers down her arm.

"There are those who would help you." It traced a rune on the back of her hand with a too-warm finger. "Many who could ease your burden. If you only accepted their–"

Lenith pushed the fey away from her, hard enough to make it stagger. It caught its balance at the top of the stairs and snarled at her. Thin lips peeled back to show black gums and rows of shark teeth.

"I'm not aligned," she pulled the tail of her shirt from her jeans and scrubbed at the back of her hand. Just in case.

"Pride yourself on that as long as you can," Thistle said. "Everyone chooses sides, soon or late. You will be no different. Either you will choose or a side will be chosen for you. Then what right will you have to look down on me?"

"That I have chosen a better master than yours." Lenith tucked her shirt back into the waistband of her jeans. "Everyone knows that the Yekum tires of Tanit's presence in his city. She is simply too arrogant to pay heed to his warnings. Soon enough, you and yours will be staked over the flames for the Yekumi's delectation. The stink of death seeps from your brand."

That punctured Thistle's bravado. It clutched its branded hand to its chest, the triangle and circle sigil of Tanit very white against its brown skin. Those who had heard what Lenith said drew back, an unsubtle distancing that left an even wider circle around Thistle. Everyone knew what Lenith had been, could be again. If anything in Even City would know death, it was her.

Thistle drew itself stiffly upright. It glared at her from under low, slanting brows, its eyes glittering furiously.

"You know nothing," it told her. "And you will regret this. Soon."

It turned and fled, in a flurry of curses and oddly jointed limbs. An uncertain silence and the smell of its rags lingered behind him. The crowd mumbled and cast her sidelong looks from the corner of their eyes. They did not seem sorry to see her go when she followed Thistle down the stairs. Creatures that lived - almost - forever had no fondness for reminders of their mortality.

Those below, who'd watched the fight from close enough they were splashed with blood, had not heard her words. They had seen her put Thistle to flight. It piqued their curiosity. They yelled questions after Lenith, some crudely framed, as she passed. There was a brittle edge to the questions. Something was coming; it hung in the air like a brewing storm, setting everyone's hair to bristling on their back on their neck. They could all feel it. It would pass, eventually.

Lenith ignored the questions, shrugging her shoulders and

The Even

waving her pale, elegant hand, and left through the side doors. The night air smelt of salt and fish. There was no reason for it to. The docks of the Even were vast and complex, with dozens of piers and storehouses, complicated pulley systems forming a lacework ceiling overhead, but there were no ships to dock there; no water lapped around the pilings. Even the whorled sand was dry.

The wind was cold against Lenith's bare face. She flipped the collar of her jacket up and pulled it closer around her, tucking her chin down into it. Her steel-toed and heeled boots clattered against the hard stone ground.

"Wait," someone called from behind her.

Lenith turned. A lanky, stoop-shouldered figure hurried after her. A Tallyman's ring of finger-length staves, each scored to mark a debt, bounced and rattled at his belt. The man was panting when he reached her. He rubbed his knuckles against his breastbone in tight, little circles. Lenith cocked her head to the side so she could make out the mark on his hand. Oeilliet's mark was drawn in blue on the back of his hand; he was contracted to the demon but not indentured.

"My debt isn't due till the third quarter of Asintmah," she said. Since time did not pass in the Even the Yekum had created one of his own. Each 'year' was divided into quarters, the passing of which was announced from the Palace, and named after one of his many children. "Tell Oelliet he will have to wait."

The Tallyman wiped his sleeve over his mouth.

"You're Lenith," he said. "I need your help."

Lenith shrugged bony shoulders.

"I don't care," she said and went to leave.

The Tallyman grabbed her arm.

"Please," he said. "Just...just listen to me. It won't take long. You won't regret it."

Lenith looked down at the hand gripping her elbow. His fingers were stained with ink and his nails were bitten down to the quick. There was a note of sweet, tarnished desperation in his voice.

"Talk then," she said, turning to face him.

The Tallyman let go her arm. He licked his lips and looked around, his eyes darting from shadow to shadow. They eventually landed back on Lenith.

"I need your help," he said.

"You said that; I told you already that I didn't care. Why should I change my mind?"

The Tallyman did another nervous scan on the street. He pulled the stave-ring from his belt and sorted through the slender, white-yew rods. The tops of each were dyed blue-purple from the ink on his fingers. He fumbled through them until he found a thin rod nearly whittled in half with debt markers. He held up.

"Your marker," he said. "If you do this, I'll break it."

If Lenith had brows that would have lifted them. If this was Oelliet's man, however temporarily, then he knew the breadth of her debt.

"Oelliet will extract the balance from your skin," she said.

The Tallyman closed his eyes. There were purple bruises in the soft skin beneath them. He swallowed hard, making his Adam's apple bob.

"I know," he croaked.

Lenith made an intrigued noise. He'd succeeded in interesting her; that, more than the promise of clearing her debt, made her nod.

"Very well," she said. "I'll listen, but that's all."

The Tallyman tucked the scored stave into his belt. He rubbed his hand over the back of his neck and looked over his shoulder. The bait was well-wrapped up now and others were following them out onto the docks. The Tallyman tucked his tongue in his cheek and shook his head.

"Not here," he said. "Somewhere private."

Lenith considered the request and nodded. She drew a square of fine linen from her shirt and looked for something to write on. All the Tallyman had was the wax tablet he recorded his bets on. Lenith shrugged and pulled the bloody Yekumi feather from her shirt. His blood had dried on it. She spat on it and scrawled a

The Even

name on the linen in a crabbed, awkward hand. The language she'd learned to write in had been shaped differently. It was easy enough for her to learn the new shapes, harder to make her fingers make them.

"Here." She tossed the fabric at him. It fluttered in the air and a gust of wind nearly carried it away. The Tallyman snatched at it and managed to catch a fraying corner between thumb and forefinger. His fingers smeared the ink. "Meet me there tonight. We can talk about it then."

The Tallyman opened the square of fabric and looked at the name on it. Kvasir's Bar. He nodded. His face was tight and strained, with deep lines scarring his skin.

"When?"

Lenith wiped the bloody feather on her sleeve and tucked it back into her shirt. The sleeve of her jacket was black and sturdily woven. The smears of the pen hardly showed on it at all.

"Tomorrow," she said. "At eighth bell."

The Tallyman shook his head violently.

"That's too late," he said. "We have to talk now."

"Tomorrow, at Kvasir," Lenith repeated gently. "Or not at all. It's your choice."

There was a pause. The Tallyman's jaw worked nervously. He touched the stave again, for reassurance, and nodded.

"Kvasir's," he said. "I'll see you there."

He turned and fled, long legs carrying him into the maze of storehouses with a bobbing, crane-like stride. Lenith watched him go till she lost track of him in the shadows.

Four

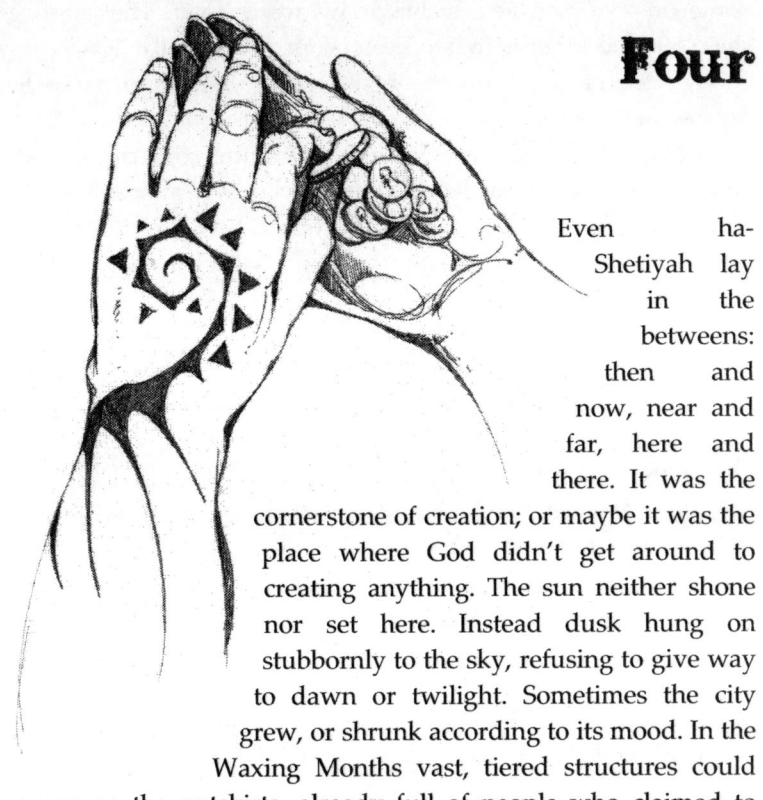

Even ha-Shetiyah lay in the betweens: then and now, near and far, here and there. It was the cornerstone of creation; or maybe it was the place where God didn't get around to creating anything. The sun neither shone nor set here. Instead dusk hung on stubbornly to the sky, refusing to give way to dawn or twilight. Sometimes the city grew, or shrunk according to its mood. In the Waxing Months vast, tiered structures could appear on the outskirts, already full of people who claimed to have been there all along, while crowded tenements would wither and die in the very heart of the city. Only the Yekum palace and the Even that anchored it was a constant.

Demons had broken ground here first; Lilith and Samael, Yekum and his mortal whores. They hid here, beyond the reach of Heaven and Hell, squatting on the Even stone whose fall would signal the End of Days. Over time the City grew and others came and settled there. Lost humans, mages, disenfranchised gods, and things seen nowhere else but here in the city, creatures of myth evicted by the spread of civilization.

They all came, made their new homes and, being what they were, started forming cadres and cabals, bargaining for souls and services. The more people who wore your rune branded, or

The Even

drawn, on their skin the more powerful you were.

Lenith wore no-one's brands.

She had lived in Even City since she had grown tired of guarding a Gate to the Deadlands that no-one used, but she had avoided bargaining away her service, freedom or essence to any of the great Lords. That made her nearly unique and, occasionally, very useful.

Five

Lenith perched on a stool by the bar, her elbow on the bone counter and her chin cupped in her hand. The blank regard of her missing face quelled the spirits of the other customers. Beings that had planned to drink from now till they were due back to work instead nursed a single brew and found excuses to leave. Usually Kvasir's Bar was full from one red wet wall to another. Tonight there was only Lenith and those few drinkers who feared nothing so much as an empty bottle.

The bartender on duty walked over and leant across the bar, fixing Lenith with eyes the colour of fresh mushrooms. There was something inescapably fungal about all the bartenders who worked and spoke for Kvasir, with their greyish skin, soft, indeterminate features and interchangeability. None of them would admit a name or had ever been seen to leave the bar. Common wisdom had it that they were grown and nurtured in the bone-raftered basements along with Kvasir's mead; no wills of their own but to be his hands and his voice.

"Buy something or leave," the bartender said. "No-one is allowed to take up a chair without drinking; besides, you're bad for business. Going around looking at people like you have the right."

Lenith twisted on the stool to face the bar and studied the stock of liquor. As well as his own mead he had bjorr, ambrosia, angel spit and demon blood. He kept a good stock in. Lenith chose something a little more pedestrian.

"Give me a bottle of whiskey." She spun a silver stater over the bar, the metal rattling against bone. "My companion tonight is human. I don't want to poison him or transport him before we speak.

The bartender shaped its soft features into a frown.

The Even

"Human," she said. "Kvasir doesn't like that sort in here. They upset his stomach."

"I'd recommend curdled mares milk for that," She said. "Now get the bottle. I don't come here for a lecture on my associates."

She lifted her hand and the silver coin had been replaced by a gold one. It would be an expensive bottle of whisky. However, either the Tallyman would take her debt, making the expense worthwhile, or he wouldn't; in which case another gold on her tallysheet was a negligible expense.

The bartender's beige eyes flickered with greed and she reached for the coin. Caution pricked before she picked it up and she paused, tilting her head back to stare up at the ceiling. A single blue eye opened over the bar, a milky glaze over iris and pupil. Kvaris was both owner and body of the bar. A dead god, grown up and over where they served his blood for a stater a pint. The process had been well underway when Lenith had first arrived in the city: bone had replaced wood and sticky clots of nerve fibres had trembled against the wall. Now there was nothing of the original bar left.

After a moment Kvaris closed his eye again. Some communication had passed between it and the bartender; she took the coin and got Lenith her bottle. Her spatulate fingers left smudges in the dust that covered the bottle

She set a wide tumbler down beside the bottle.

"If he makes trouble, any trouble, he goes out," she said. "You with him."

Lenith inclined her head.

"Understood," she said.

The bartender stared at her without blinking for a long moment. Finally she nodded.

"Make sure you do," she said. "I'll be watching."

Someone yelled for service at the other end of the bar, banging a tankard insistently on the counter.

It did little to ruffle the bartender's composure. She just nodded an acknowledgement of the order and headed down the bar, collecting a jar of mean from a shelf on her way past.

Lenith picked up the bottle and pried the cork free from the neck. Without bothering to wipe the glass she filled it with whiskey. Particles of dust floated on top of the honey-amber liquid. She idly dipped her finger into it and stirred it. The dust swirled around her fingers. She lifted her finger out, drops falling from the tip, and started to draw on the bar. Damp lines etched out words and sentences in the old alphabet on the weathered leather bone. These shapes came easily to her fingers. She only managed to write two sentences before the bartender put a heavy, callused hand on top of hers. It felt dry and yielding, with no sense of bones under the coating of flesh.

"Don't."

"It means nothing," Lenith said. She flexed her fingers, but the bartender was stronger than she appeared. "They are just doodles."

"I still don't like it; neither does anyone else." The bartender pressed down, flattening Lenith's hand against the cold bone. "So..."

Where the eye had been, a thin-lipped mouth opened, lipping against the ceiling. Spit formed in the corners and dripped to the ground and onto the customers. They cringed and moved to the side, scraping the legs of their chairs over the floor. No-one protested. Kvasir was, dead or not, a god.

"Stop." The bar and bartender said the word at the same time. It was hard to tell which mouth was mirroring which.

There was silence. Then Lenith dipped her chin.

"Very well," she said. The bartender raised her hand and Lenith pulled hers free. She swept it over the bar. Her palm smeared the elegant words into a smear of glistening, amber liquid. "I don't want to cause any problems."

The bartender stared at her and then laughed, a sound that had no relation to the deadpan expression on her face. Overhead the mouth moved around the same sound.

"More comfort," they said, "if you did not find it so easy to lie with a straight face, Lenith."

"It's a help." Lenith rubed the stickiness of the alcohol from her

The Even

hand. "But I'm not lying. I don't plan on trouble tonight.

"Then trouble will find you." The bartender pointed a finger at Lenith, still speaking Kvasir's words. "It's not my place to judge, but you are a thing of the Deadlands and should never have left. In the lands above you're a stormcrow for trouble."

She walked away without waiting for an answer and the mouth overhead faded back into the ceiling. It was for the best. They were probably right and Lenith had no skill for finding comforting lies. She had never needed to learn; the dead were beyond comfort.

The great bells of the Palace rang the turning of the hour. There was no sun, so the whole city judged the time by the peals of those bells. Lenith shifted around on the stool so she could see the door. Her finger tapped a steady rhythm against the bar. The Tallyman was verging on being late.

Two drunken Kulshedra staggered in, laughing, with their bloody arms linked and their body hair braided and tinkling with charms. They bought a bottle of Kvasir's own mead to share. Later a pack of kobolds, their tails crooked over their backs and eyes glittering, tumbled in through the door. They split up and darted through the bar, spindly fingers getting everywhere.

The bartender caught up a long, curved white bone, the rib of a titan, and jabbed it at them, poking them away from the bar. They spat insults at her in their own tongue and skipped along the bar. Lenith caught her glass and bottle and lifted them out of the way of their dirty feet. The bartender caught one of them a solid blow with her stick, sweeping its feet from under it. It somersaulted off the bar and landed flat on its back on the ground, dazed and wheezing. The rest of the pack retreated, collecting their fallen mate, and fled the bar, hissing imprecations over their shoulders.

"Vermin," the bartender said, glaring after them. She tucked the rib safely away under the bar and started to count the bottles of liquor.

Just before Lenith's patience expired the Tallyman slunk into the room. His tall, thin frame fell in on itself; his shoulders tucked in, collapsing his chest, and his back was hunched. The tally-ring still hung off his belt. He blinked watery, nervous eyes around the room, his gaze shying from the Kulshedra. When he saw Lenith some sort of tension bled visibly from him and he shrugged out of his jacket on the way over to join her.

"You waited," he said.

"Just." Lenith put her finger against the base of the glass and pushed it towards him. "Talk."

The man reached for the glass, hesitated and then picked it up. He tossed back half the glass in one mouthful and gasped when it hit the back of his throat. Tears formed in his eyes. He finished the glass and wiped his eyes with his knuckle, mumbling something to God as he did so. It was wasted breath. No gods held sway here, no demons either. There was just the Yekum whims.

Lenith refilled his glass when he set it down, right to the very top. He reached for it again, his fingers shaking, but Lenith put her hand on top of it.

"You said you needed my help," she reminded him.

The Tallyman wiped his unbranded hand over the back of his mouth, stretching his lips to reveal singed gums, and nodded.

"Yes. I…" he looked around. His eyes lingered on the wet walls and he shuddered. He stepped closer to Lenith and dropped his voice. "Is it safe to talk here?"

"It is for me."

The Tallyman's mouth twitched. He looked around and then slid his narrow hips onto stool. His bony knees poked out at sharp angles, pressing against the faded fabric of his trews. He jerked at the cuffs on his jerkin, fiddling with the ties.

"I'm here on behalf of my patron," he said.

Lenith reached over and touched the brand on the back of his hand. She could feel the vibration in the ink, the net of debt and obligation and servitude that thrummed against her skin and that the Tallyman was tied into until the ink faded from his skin.

"Oelliet?"

The Tallyman pulled his hand away and covered the brand with his hand. His fingers tightened, his knuckles showing white through tanned skin.

The Even

"No. My real patron. The demon just employs me."

As if there was a difference here. Humans sometimes seemed unable to accept the reality of what the brands were. As if selling yourself somehow had more honour than being sold.

"Who's your true patron then?" she asked.

The Tallyman grimaced and rubbed the back of his hand.

"That I cannot tell you," he said. "She must remain anonymous. For her own safety no-one can know of her involvement. That is one thing that is not negotiable."

Lenith lifted her hand off the glass.

"Go on," she said.

He grabbed the glass, fingers clutching it tight, and took another drink. A dribble of whiskey ran down his chin. He wiped it away on his sleeve.

"You aren't going to refuse?" he asked, like he'd thought she would.

Lenith shifted, leaning her back against the counter, and crossed her legs. She laced her fingers together around her knee. Then she was still, composed and waiting.

"You haven't bored me yet," she said. "Until you do, I'll listen. But my attention moves on swiftly; so speak your piece."

The Tallyman wiped his mouth again and took a deep breath, swelling his pigeon chest.

"My patron wants to contract your services in return for buying off your debt," he said quickly. "If you perform one service for us, Oelliet will have no hold on you. That's what my patron offers."

Lenith looked down at the ring on his belt. She couldn't pick out which scored rod was the tally of her debt. There were many deeply marked with debt.

"How kind of them."

The Tallyman's lips thinned. "Do you accept the deal or not?"

Lenith shook her head. The Tallyman opened his mouth to say something. She held up her hand, unlined palm towards him, to forestall whatever it was.

"No. I will not bind myself to anything; not until I know what your patron desires. Being rid of my debt is not worth getting killed, or worse."

"Worse?"

"Oh there's worse than dying. Dying isn't that bad," Lenith said. The Tallyman just grunted and shook his head. He was newcome to the city, and naïve, if he thought death was the worst that could be done to him.

There was a rattle of bone on bone. Lenith shifted so she could see over the Tallyman's shoulder. Two men were playing a dice game at a nearby table. One scooped up the dice from the table and shook them quickly. He jerked his wrist and threw them onto the table. The dice, cubes of bone with the edges rounded off and marks scratched onto each surface, rolled over the table. One hit a tankard and bounced backwards. They came up skulls, a crude sketch with two crossed lines for eyes, and the man hissed in triumph. The other man closed his eyes and dropped his head.

Luck, chaos. It fascinated her. Death was inevitable, and thus predictable.

Her attention stayed on the lizard, watching him scrape up his winnings, while she spoke to the Tallyman.

"So, tell me. What do you want?"

The loser from the dice game got up and stumbled up to the bar. He braced his arms on the counter and ordered a bottle of wine. From the drawn look to his face he'd finish it tonight. The Tallyman had been about to say something. He snapped his jaw shut and shook his head.

"I can't tell you here," he said. "It wouldn't be safe, for either of us."

Lenith didn't move until the Tallyman shifted again, his fingers tightening around the glass.

"Very well." She slid off the stool and tugged her jacket straight. "We can talk outside. Bring the whiskey. I paid for it."

She walked out of the bar without waiting to see if he followed. Outside the dusk had deepened, purple shadows poured into the corners of building, and Lenith stuck her hands into her jacket pockets. The lined leather made a soft, organic sound as it pulled

The Even

down over her shoulders. She looked around, turned left and walked away briskly. Long legs carried her down the street, against the flow of traffic.

She turned left at the corner and walked down a narrow alley. Mud and fouler things squelched underfoot. A raggedly dressed fiddler stood in the middle of the alley, his back against the wall and his face turned skyward. His eyes were closed and his face slack with concentration. He was engrossed in his music, swaying and sawing his bow over the string.

The Tallyman caught up with her at the corner, pushing his way between two aged, gnarled beings whose sex had long since become indeterminate. One of them spat at his heel.

"You said you'd listen," he reminded her, one hand pressed against his chest.

"I will," Lenith said. She shifted her weight onto one leg, standing hipshot and casual. "We can talk here."

The Tallyman stared at her.

"What about..." He stopped and jerked his head towards the fiddler.

"Tom?" Lenith shook her head, her dreads whispering against each other. "He can't hear us. Or if he can, he can't tell any tales. You've heard the tales of people challenging the Devil, for riches and wealth and talent? Well, they don't always win."

The Tallyman rubbed his hand over his mouth. "Oh," he said softly.

"Yes. Tom here hasn't stopped playing in a..." Lenith paused to tally the years up in her head. "A century or so. I doubt he will start now to repeat your secrets. Which you are about to tell me?"

The Tallyman stared at Tom suspiciously. The fiddler didn't even acknowledge their existence. To him there was nothing in the world but the music. Blood welled from under his fingertips and dripped into the fiddle-case that lay open at his feet. It stained the pale, silk linen rust.

"My patron wants you to find someone," the Tallyman said finally.

Lenith turned her attention away from the music and towards

T.A. Moore

the Tallyman. Her voice sharpened with a hint of impatience. "That's the secret you couldn't tell me in the bar? I think you may be starting to bore me, Tallyman."

"No. Of course that's not it, it's…" He stopped to let a woman in a white dress walk past their station. She paused long enough to drop a copper into the case. Then she went on about her way. The Tallyman waited until she was well out of earshot before finishing his sentence. "The secret is who she wants you to find."

"And that would be?"

The Tallyman breathed in and dried his sweaty hands on his thighs.

"The Unnamed," he said. "She wants you to bring back the Unnamed from the Deathlands."

Sx

The only way into the Even Palace, unless you had wings, was to climb the Stairway of a Thousand Steps.

Each step was carved of black marble and dipped in the middle, worn down by the footsteps of centuries of supplicants. It leads into the Hall of Names, the only part of the city most of the common citizens ever see. To venture further, into the upper levels of the Palace where the Yekumi Kin-lines live, required strict vetting by the Palace Guard. And those selected did not return unchanged.

Thin sheets of ivory sheathed the stone wall of the Hall. Each sheet was covered with runes, telling the history of the city. It started by the door, telling the story of how the Even had first been found, and continued nearly to the throne.

The throne was carved from a giant tooth, a molar ripped from the jaw of one of the beasts that used to haunt these lands, and set on a high dais. On either side of it the walls were still being carved. Artisans, skin blackened and eyes burned white from bathing in the glory of the Yekum, crouched there day and night. They scratched the deeds of the city onto the wall as they happened, using styluses made from their own fingerbones.

Each artisan was chained to the large, leather-bound book that stood on a stone lectern in the middle of the Hall. The Book contained the name of every citizen that resided in the city, runes burnt onto the still-living pages. Yekum's rune was a circle with an arrow piercing the side. The rune of the notorious City-bred thief Jack consisted of three curved lines that, together, gave the impression of a dagger. Some runes, like Yekum's appeared over and over again on the walls. Others were seen rarely. Every name was represented at least once. There was not a single soul in the city that was overlooked by the Yekum.

T.A. Moore

Occasionally the artisans shuffled over to the book and closed it. They'd trace the sore edges of the single rune branded on the cover with their pared down finger-bones. Once it was memorised they'd return to the wall and erase a name, replacing it with the cover rune.

In doing so they unnamed the person, unmade them and cast them off. All debts to that person, all bonds and deals and bloodlines, are null and void.

It is a rarely used punishment, and dangerous.

The Even

 Seven

Lenith stepped away from the wall. The wise thing to do would be to leave and pretend this conversation had never taken place. Instead she paced a wide circle around Tom and stopped in front of the Tallyman. She stepped closer, edging into his personal space.

"The Unnamed?" she asked. He nodded mutely. "Why?"

"That I can't tell you. Just that if you do it your debts will be paid off. In full."

Lenith shook her head and stepped back. The Tallyman stepped after her, mouth already open in an attempt to convince her.

"Be silent," she told him. "Let me think."

"But..."

"If I decide right now, the answer is no," Lenith said. "Do you want me to decide?"

The Tallyman pressed his lips together, so tight they turned white, and shook his head. His thinning brown hair trailed over his shoulders. Lenith waited but he stayed mute. She nodded her approval and walked a few feet down the alley.

Her debts, and her habits, had weighed on her shoulders since her arrival in the city. That had been centuries ago; both debt and habits grew a little with each year. Sometimes she had a run of good luck and paid off her debts. More often the luck ran against her and her debt-stave was whittled thin. Either way, Lenith went on her way regardless.

It would be tempting to be able to pay off her markers. Not tempting enough to associate herself with a mission that would anger the Yekumi. Their wrath was slow-burning and expressed in odd, cruel ways. One woman, who had unwisely boasted she was more beautiful than one of the Yekum's children, still hung in their gallery. Her skin had been flayed from her bones and mounted in a frame, pinned with silver nails. She still lived, her eyes rolling and her mouth moving silently; they hadn't left her a tongue.

Coin could not off-set the danger of ending up like that. Oelliet would not kill or maim her, not permanently. He wanted her coin in his pocket, besides, as she'd pointed out once before, when staters were hard to come by, all killing her would do was send her home.

The puzzle was a different matter. There was something brewing in the city that she didn't know about. Of course, there was much that happened in the city she didn't know about, that she wasn't interested in. This, though, had brought itself to her attention. It seemed ungrateful to turn it away.

Immortality grew dull over the years. There were only so many sunrises that would delight; only so many meals that would make a mouth water. Even sex grew uninspiring after the five thousandth time.

After that new forms of distraction had to be found. A vice whose outcome you could not control — the rattle of dice and the silent straining of gladiators — or a virtue whose attainment was beyond your grasp.

Lenith turned, her heel grinding into the mud, and walked back to the Tallyman. He chewed nervously on the end of his thumbnail, peeling shreds of skin from his thumb.

"You want to free the Unnamed," she said. "The young treacher."

The Tallyman nodded sharply. His chin bumped against his breastbone. Lenith ran her fingers through her hair and stared at him.

No one loved the Yekumi. They ruled by precedent and might. So who would go to such lengths to reclaim this one? Only another Yekumi cared what happened to their kin, but the treacher had been convicted of conspiring against his own. None of them had even come to witness his fate, why risk sharing it by going against the Yekum?

T.A. Moore

Lenith turned the questions over in her head while the Tallyman fidgeted and Tom played. She snapped her fingers to catch the Tallyman's attention.

"Why me? This Master of yours has servants of her own, surely."

"None of whom are Lenith."

Lenith crossed her arms. "Obviously."

"The Lilim's Curse took the Unnamed to the Deathlands," he said. "You were a goddess of the dead. If anyone can find him, you can."

"There are others in the city who dwelt below. Urshanabi, Orpheus…" She shrugged. "Not many but some."

"None who spent as long there as you and they are all branded." The Tallyman gestured at Lenith's hands and the bare line of her neck. She never sold her skin. "They can be watched."

Tom finished his song and started to play 'Under the Well in the Valley'. Lenith listened to him, tapping her foot in time to the dark little tune. The Tallyman waited as long as he could, then he cleared his throat.

"Well? What is your answer?"

Lenith listened to a few more chords of 'Under the Well' and then she nodded.

"I will find the Unnamed," she said.

They shook on it. Lenith squeezed his hand and felt the weight of the deal settling itself in her bones. Good idea or not, she was bound to this now.

"When I find him," she asked. "What will I do with him?"

The Tallyman pulled his hand free. He flexed his fingers and rubbed at the ache in his palm.

"Bring him back to the city, back from the Deathlands," he said. An expression of, almost, fear flickered over his face. He looked at her sharply. "You can do that, can't you?"

Lenith let a beat of silence pass before she answered.

"It's possible," she said.

He nodded, sighing in relief, and didn't notice she hadn't quite answered his question. It was possible; that didn't mean it could

The Even

be done.

"Bring him back," he repeated. "Then contact me. I'll tell you what to do from there. Then you'll forget we ever asked this of you; that you ever even thought of doing it. Do you understand?"

He stared at her, more confident now that she'd taken the deal. Their status, in his head, reversed; he was in control and she, the petitioner. Humans and the little status-games they played. It made them so easy sometimes.

Lenith shrugged elegantly.

"I understand what you're asking," she said. "And that you have no power to enforce it. A word of advice, little debt-taker, this is Even City: demons and angels and monsters and things that never made it as far as your little plane walk the streets here. We are ruled by the Yekum's whim and the City's one, unbreakable law: a deal is a deal. If you wish to add riders then you do it before the deal is made."

The Tallyman pulled himself up and squared his shoulders, still hiding behind his assumed control. He stuck his chin out at her pugnaciously.

"If you don't abide by our terms, then the deal's off," he said. "Your debt-stave stays intact."

Lenith chuckled; a low, rich, joyous sound. A bird dropped from the gutter overhead and landed in the alley: dead. The Tallyman flinched and the last of his assumed confidence drained away. His shoulders tented inwards again.

"You don't welch on deals in the Even," Lenith told him. "That's why Oelliet doesn't need collectors. The city has its own ways of enforcing its will. I'll bring the treacher back; you'll fulfil your end of the bargain, or you'll find out what is worse than death here."

The Tallyman looked down at his muddy feet, his eyelid fluttering at the corner.

"No-one can know of my Patron's involvement," he said. It was a plea rather than a demand. "It will ruin her if they do. She is... high in the Palace. If the Yekum finds out she has gone against him..."

"Then be at ease," Lenith said. "I have yet to find cause to speak to the Yekum. Nor do I wish him to know of my role in this. There's no benefit to me in exposing this secret."

She still hadn't promised anything, but the Tallyman caught at her words like she had. He swallowed hard and nodded, looking relieved.

"Thank you," he said. "Do you need anything?"

Lenith walked away from him, stepping over the dead bird.

"From you?" she said over her shoulder. "No. Nothing."

She left him standing there in the alley, a dead bird at his feet and his arms hanging limp from his shoulders. Tom played on, heedless of what went on around him.

Lenith took the long way through the city. She wanted to give her thoughts time to settle.

The Unnamed, the Yekumi curse and the mysterious patron who was willing, and able, to pay a substantial amount, for Lenith's debts were no small thing, for the return of the Unnamed; they all troubled her. She couldn't quite see how they fit together.

The uncertainty was marvellous.

She turned left at the statue of Grendel's mother, her great form bent in grief over her one-armed son, and headed down into the tenements. There were cobblestones under her feet instead of smooth pavement. The streets were narrow and washing lines, strung from the upper windows, formed a net overhead. Sheets and bright-hued sweaters flapped furiously in the wind, about to take flight.

A small face appeared at one of the windows and licked the glass with a long, black tongue.

Lenith took a left into Clootie Alley and stopped sharply. There was a rough brick wall blocking the way. It hadn't been there the last time she'd come this way.

The tenements were a maze of crossroads and dead-ends. They were the most heavily populated areas in the city and were rarely cannibalised for new buildings or areas. They were fluid, however. Streets moved overnight or became cul-de-sacs and occasionally transported themselves from one side of the city to

The Even

the other.

Or walls appeared from nowhere.

Lenith took a step back. The wall was covered in graffiti and posters already.

'The Princes of Fear are watching,' was scrawled in small, tight lettering at an angle across the top of the wall.

A Fifth Men leaflet was stuck to the bricks. The paper was sodden with glue and the ink had smeared, blurring the lettering.

'Senoi Sansenoi Sammangelof' was written in a circle in the middle of the wall, the f and s hooked around each other to anchor the charm.

'Boli Shah,' had been written in bubbles of pink and green and then angrily scored out.

In the very middle of the wall

someone had drawn the rune for Dust, a Y dissected with two lines. It also meant Nameless and it was the rune used in the Unnaming. Lenith touched the rune. It was still wet.

She drew her hand back and rubbed her fingers together. The paint felt oily and gritty against her skin. Blood and ashes.

"Damnation," a broken voice said, two harmonies fighting with each other. Lenith turned and wiped her hand down her leg. A bird-man with great, iridescent broken wings stood behind her. "The streets aren't staying the same from one day to the next this weather."

"It's been worse than usual?" she asked.

The man clicked his beak together and shrugged, his wings making a dry, rustling sound. The bones poked out through the skin at the joints, just visible through the bloody feathers.

"A bit. We lost part of Sulphur Crescent last night." He held a hand up and scissored his fingers together. "Snipped right off in the middle of the night. Hope they come back. Old Yusha owed me money."

The thought made his blue-

The Even

barred feathers fluff. Then he slicked them back down. He pointed at the wall with his hooked beak.

"If you're looking for the other side of Clootie Alley you can take a short-cut through Dee Street. It should still be there."

Lenith nodded to him.

"Thanks."

He shrugged, dropping feathers, and left. Lenith took a last thoughtful look at the wall and then followed his directions. The short-cut down Dee Street lead her to the missing half of Clootie Alley. It was grafted onto Ishtar Square, tucked uncomfortably between two small, neat houses with brightly coloured window boxes.

There was a puddle of oil-smeared water in the mouth of the alley. Lenith stepped over it — her distorted reflection trapped briefly — and walked up to a peeling, green door. She knocked it three times.

After a second she heard the door unlatch.

"Come in," a low, throaty voice said.

Lenith put her hand flat against the door and pushed it open, the hinges creaking. She ducked her head under the lintel and stepped inside. It was dark on the other side of the door; the only light came from the fire that smouldered in the grate. A bubbling pot hung over the fire. A shawled, voluptuous woman sat in front of the fire, tending the pot.

"You should lock the door," Lenith said. She walked over to the hearth and dropped into a crouch opposite the woman. The fire scalded the half of her body that faced it.

The woman pushed her shawl back from her head. Silvered black hair slid free and fell over her round shoulders. She smirked with thick, red lips.

"No one would steal from me, Gatekeeper. They know better than to cross Mother Blight." She leant forwards and stirred the pot, mixing the grease into the stew. Gobbets of meat floated to the surface, rolled and sank again. Mother Blight tapped the ladle against the side of the pot and hung it up from the hearth. "Sooner or later, they all have need of me. Just like you, Gatekeeper. That is why you've come visiting, isn't it?"

"I need to know about the curse," Lenith said.

Mother Blight looked down at her and raised a dark, well-shaped eyebrow.

"And what curse would that be? The curse Old Clutterbuck put on the grocer who short-changed her or the dose of the Evil Eye I gave to Mary Blee's son for pissing in my garden? This is the city, Gatekeeper, there are curses on every corner."

Lenith laced her hands together over her knees.

"Not a curse," she said. "The Curse, the Yekumi curse. What do you know about it?"

Mother Blight pursed her lips. She picked up the ladle and stirred the pot, giving her time to think.

"You'll pay for the information?" she asked.

"Of course," Lenith said. She reached into her pocket and pulled out a gold stater, holding it up between her fingers. Mother Blight grunted and sat back on the stool. Her pipe lay on top of the hearth. She reached up and lifted it down, tamping tobacco into the bowl with a herb stained thumb. Then she lit it with a snap of her fingers and placed the pipe into her mouth. Her cheeks hollowed around it as she puffed. It smouldered, giving off threads of pale blue smoke. Mother Blight's ash-dark eyes studied Lenith through the hovering pall. "You know the details of the curse itself, of course?"

"I'm not paying you to listen to me talk."

"Fair enough," Mother Blight said. She drew deeply on the pipe, coughed and spat on the ground. "A hundred years ago one of the Lilim cursed the Yekumi."

"Why?"

The Even

"No-one knows actually. The Lilim are… unpredictable. They share their dam's hatred for being told what to do. Perhaps the Yekum had outraged her and she wanted revenge. Or it might have been a prank on the Yekumi: a deadly one." She paused and looked expectantly. Lenith just waited. When no question was forthcoming Mother Blight cleared her throat and continued with her story. "The Lilim's motivation might have been clouded but her curse was clear enough. You know the wording as well as me; she cursed all the parts of them and summoned the spirits of the earth to enforce the spell. So whenever a Yekumi sets foot to earth, the gnomes, the Earth Spirits, kill them. It was a simple spell, but effective; elegant really."

Lenith ignored the moment of professional courtesy. She leant forwards, the waistband of her jeans digging into her stomach. "Kills?"

"As good as." Mother Blight took the pipe from her mouth, the stem wet with spit, and gestured dismissively with it. "They take them away to the Deathlands."

"But the gnomes don't kill them," Lenith pressed. "They are taken alive?"

Mother Blight shrugged, her full breasts moving under her loose gown.

"They are," she said. "Thought it does them little good, I'm sure. None of them have returned."

"So far," Lenith murmured to herself. She scratched the back of her hand with her thumbnail. "Who cast the spell?"

Mother Blight took the pipe from her mouth. She blew on the smouldering herbs, making the fire glow.

"I don't know," she admitted reluctantly. "I could scry for the answers but that would not be…"

"Safe?"

"Wise." The witch gave an offended huff. She sucked on the pipe again, filling her lungs with smoke, and blew it out towards the ceiling. The smoke collected there, clinging to the rafters. "And that is all I know of the curse, Gatekeeper."

"What happens to the Yekumi?"

T.A. Moore

Mother Blight frowned. She shifted on the stool and adjusted her skirts, shaking the folds loose and smoothing them down over her thighs.

"Why do you want to know?" she asked.

Lenith hitched her shoulders in a shrug.

"I'm not the one being paid for answers." She stood up. The smoke eddied around her pale hair. She was sweating from the heat of the fire. Her shirt was clinging to her stomach and breasts. She tugged it free of her skin. "Answer the question."

Mother Blight looked sour. But, despite her annoyance, she was intrigued by the question. She tapped the stem of her pipe against her stained teeth while she considered the question.

"Bear in mind, this is speculation," she said. Lenith nodded. There was another pause while Mother Blight organised her thoughts. "The living have gone to the Deathlands and returned before. To go there is not fatal. The Yekumi are taken alive and they are not easily killed. It is reasonable to assume they live still, as prisoners of the gnomes. The Earth Elementals dwell on the same plane and they are covetous. Once something was theirs, they would not easily surrender it."

Lenith nodded.

"I know." She handed the golden stater to Mother Blight, dropping it into the old witch's stained palm. Then she drew a full silver from her pocket and held it up. The firelight glittered on the metal. Mother Blight reached for it but Lenith refused to relinquish it to her. "This is not for the information. I need to buy some things from you."

Mother Blight's white, lush features crinkled in disappointment. She let go of the coin.

"What do you want?" she asked.

"A bag of salt from your larder, some bones from your stew and," Lenith released the coin "your silence."

"I don't gossip about my customers, Gatekeeper, no one would ask for their philtres and curses from me anymore if I did." Mother Blight got up, grunting as she straightened her back, and rubbed the small of her back. She went over the cabinet and

The Even

opened it, lifting out a grubby white bag. "Do you want the whole bag?"

"Yes," Lenith said.

Mother Blight twisted the mouth of the bag in her broad, capable hands. She nodded at the pot over the fire.

"Get your own bones," she said.

Lenith stepped up the fire, her toes touching the stone of the hearth, and looked into the pot. A thick film of grease floated on the top of bubbling liquid. Unidentifiable chunks of bone and meat floated and turned. Lenith pushed her sleeve up to her elbow. She thrust her hand into the pot. The water scalded her skin and cooked the flesh. She groped at the bottom of the pot. Meat slid through her fingers, slimy and slippery. She gathered up a handful of bones and lifted them from the pot. Her fingers were scalded a dark, hurtful red. They faded quickly, turning from red to pink. By the time she turned her hand over, opening her fingers, they were healed.

Out of the bones she had plucked from the stew she chose three knucklebones and tossed the rest back into the pot. They splashed into the stew.

Lenith pulled her shirt out of her jeans and dried the bones. She checked them for cracks and tucked them into her pocket. Her hands were greasy from the stew. She wiped them on her thighs.

"I'd wish you luck but I doubt it would do any good," Mother Blight said, depositing the sack of salt in Lenith's hands. She sat back down in front of the fire and lifted the long ladle. She stirred the stew and dipped out a ladleful to sniff. Her nostrils flared and her lips parted. "Nearly ready. Close the door on your way out. I don't want the babe to grow chilled."

Lenith tucked the salt into the bend of her arm. She inclined her head to Mother Blight.

"My thanks for your help," she said.

Mother Blight looked up and stared, narrow-eyed, at Lenith.

"I suspect my help will bring you no joy," she said. "But I wish you well."

From the pot a scrawny creature of bone stitched together with

T.A. Moore

stringy sinew and cobwebs crawled, claw over claw, and mewled demandingly. Mother Blight held her hands out for it to tumble into and cradled it to her full, black-nippled breast. It found the nipple with a razor-toothed maw and suckled hungrily at her blood.

Lenith closed the door behind her with a firm click.

Eight

Graveyards were unquiet places in the city. The graves are weighed down with blocks of granite, each etched with sealing words and the names of the dead. Ragged X's, scrawled in blood and paint both, marked the gravestones. Shrines were painstakingly constructed in front of many of the graves: thin candles, pools of multi-coloured, melted wax and little offers of sweets and small, eviscerated animals. They could be designed to either placate what lay under the earth or to call it up.

Poles, strung with hanks of red and green cloth, mark the safe places between the graves. It is never empty. There are always people there: mourners and gloaters, thieves and grave robbers. The latter are scarred from their dangerous profession, many missing limbs or eyes, too. Sometimes, in the city, what is buried isn't necessarily dead.

Lenith found it a restful place.

She squatted down next to an ancient grave. The sealing runes and sigils were worn nearly smooth and the stones holding the corpse down were cracked. Lenith dropped the dirty sack of salt onto the ground. She pulled a switchblade from her pocket; the handle made of scrimshawed bone, and popped the blade. It was thin and the honed edge was coated with silver, sharp enough to cut the air. Lenith used it to gut the salt bag, steel ripping through rough canvas with a loud, organic sound. Salt spilled from the wound like blood. It coated the ground and stuck to Lenith's fingers. She tore the canvas roughly into quarters and parcelled them up into small, rough bags. A handful of salt and a handful dirt from the old thing's grave went into each bag, then Lenith tied it up with a piece of cured leather. Each bag was about the size of her closed fist.

Lenith moved the bones from her jacket to the pocket of her jeans. Then the bags of salt went into her jacket, weighting it down over her shoulders. She left the salt on the ground to be blown away or walked into the dirt. What she had would serve her purpose.

There were many tracks and trails in the graveyard. They all led to the hill in the centre of the plot, where the four main roads met. At the crossroads a huge mausoleum had been erected. It bulked grimly over the graveyard, a house of the dead built on the same scale as those of the living. There was a stone gargoyle on

The Even

the roof, frozen in an attempt to take flight. Legend had it that it would finally tear its way free just in time for the End of Days. There was the lintel and frame of a door, but where the door should be there was just blank, grey stone. Two angels, one goat-headed and the other two-faced, guarded the walled up entrance with bared swords.

Lenith stepped through the gate and walked up the path, the stone mortared with blood and bone-dust. She stopped between the two angels. Cold radiated from the door, making her shiver and rub her hands together.

When she touched the stone it was hard, impermeable. The way was blocked. Her bones ached from the cold.

There was always one way through. Lenith drew her switchblade again. She sliced the heel of her hand open, pressing down so the blade sank down to the bone. Blood poured from the cut. Lenith tipped her hand so the blood pooled in her palm and dipped her finger into it. Then she painted her name on the door in a few, ragged lines.

The blood glistened and slowly sank into the stone. When the last of it disappeared the stone creaked and then cracked slowly open. The opening was just wide enough to let her enter. Tendrils of thick, grey mist spilled out over the ground, tangling around Lenith's feet. They tugged at her. Lenith checked her pockets one last time: salt, bones, coins and a stub of chalk she'd taken from a grave. Everything you needed for a visit to the Deathlands. She took one last look at the city and squeezed through the door. The edges caught over her breasts. She had to hollow her chest and pull herself free.

On the other side of the door the thick mist eddied around her. It stroked her face and wound damply and affectionately through her hair.

It was glad to see she was back. Home, again.

Lenith walked forwards slowly, careful of her footing on the treacherous path, and eventually the mist started to clear. She could hear a river and the low moans of the newly dead. The mist thickened in front of Lenith's face, turning almost solid. She

T.A. Moore

pushed her way forwards, holding up a hand to part the grey wall.

Finally she stepped free of the mists and looked down over a sere, rocky vista full of boulders and pits. A dark river flowed sluggishly through the landscape, so wide the far bank was hard to see. There was neither night nor day here. Instead there was a sullen, reddish light that could have been stolen from either the dawn or death of the sun. But there was heat. It cracked the yellow rocks and turned the earth to dust.

Nine

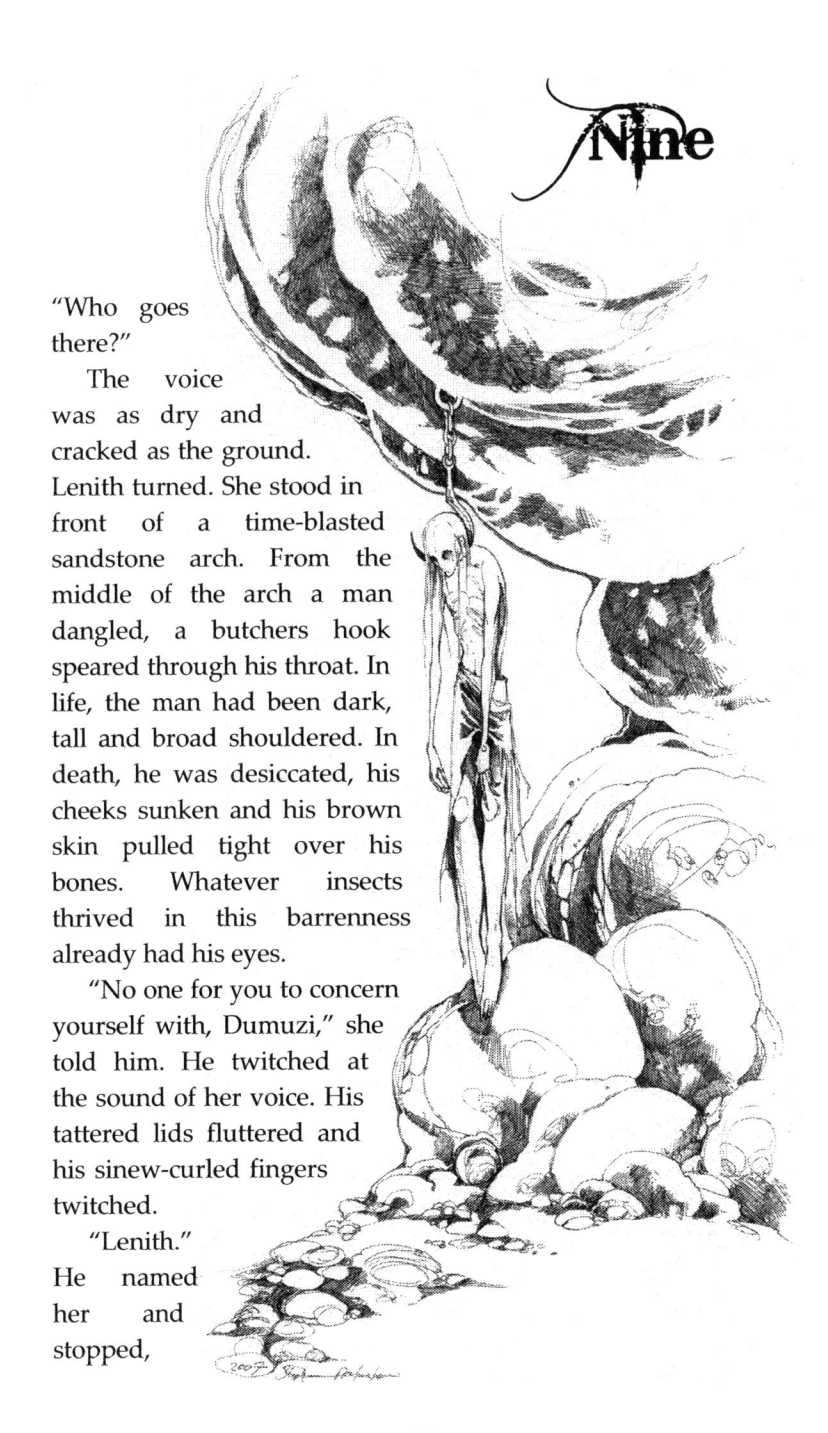

"Who goes there?"

The voice was as dry and cracked as the ground. Lenith turned. She stood in front of a time-blasted sandstone arch. From the middle of the arch a man dangled, a butchers hook speared through his throat. In life, the man had been dark, tall and broad shouldered. In death, he was desiccated, his cheeks sunken and his brown skin pulled tight over his bones. Whatever insects thrived in this barrenness already had his eyes.

"No one for you to concern yourself with, Dumuzi," she told him. He twitched at the sound of her voice. His tattered lids fluttered and his sinew-curled fingers twitched.

"Lenith." He named her and stopped,

struggling to fill his lungs. Air hissed through the hole in his throat. His sunken chest swelled, cracking the skin under his ribs, and he forced the words out on a long exhalation. "Have you returned...to your empty duties, then?"

Lenith put her hand on his leg. It felt warm and hard, like dried leather. She gave him a push, setting him to spinning. The hook ripped his throat more but his body was too dry to give any more blood up. It hadn't always been so. The ground beneath his toes was filthy black with bloodstains.

"My empty duties?" she mocked. "Your only duty is to hang there and rot in your wife's place, Dumuzi. Your unfaithful wife."

The corpse groaned, a low, keening ululation. Lenith let him swing for a while before she grabbed his foot and stopped him. The keening went on. She pitched her voice to carry over it.

"Has anyone passed by here in the last few days, Dumuzi?"

Dumuzi shook his head, the gesture canted due to the hook.

"Why should I tell you?" he asked.

"Why not?" Lenith said. Dumuzi curled a dried lip in a sneer. She shrugged and offered, in a dulcety sweet voice, "I could always get you down from your hook?"

Dumuzi laughed raggedly.

"And where would I go?" he asked. "My place here is ordained; it cannot be changed. I will not desert my people."

Lenith shook her head; his people had abandoned him long ago. His funerary rites had not been performed in centuries. He would never accept that, though.

"Then what can I offer?" she asked.

Dumuzi licked at his lips with a twisted, hardened tongue. It looked more like a bit of jerky than anything else.

"Water," he said. "Get me a drink, Lenith of the Etrusci. Get me a drink and I will tell you what I know."

Lenith half-turned. The river was not far away. It would not take her long to walk there and return. Besides, there was no time-limit placed on her task.

"Very well." She gave him a push, just enough to make him swing gently. "But if I uphold my side of the bargain and you tell

The Even

me that you know nothing. I will be...unhappy."

The choice of words made Dumuzi laugh, hitching, raw sounds that tore out of his chest. They were almost convulsions and they jerked his body, making him swing harder. The hook widened the hole in his throat.

"Unhappy," he said. "An emotion I am more than familiar with. Fetch me the water, Lenith. I will tell you what I know."

He let his head drop, his chin resting on the hook, and said no more.

Lenith walked down towards the river. The thought of helping the other god galled her, he was a relic and a fool clinging to duties he knew were meaningless, but she needed what he knew. All who entered the Deathlands passed through that arch, under Dumuzi's empty eyes.

Halfway down the slope she slipped. She landed hard on the ground and slid down, grabbing at rocks and roots to slow her fall. It started a miniature avalanche, with stones and pebbles rolling down the hill and splashing into the river. A root slid through Lenith's fingers. Then she caught hold of a deeply buried rock and stopped her fall; although it felt like she had nearly dislocated her shoulder.

The noise attracted some of the dead and they came drifting up the hill: pale, vague people in pleated linen. The women wore their hair in braids; the men wore their beards oiled and curled. Smears of makeup from their burial still stained their eyes and mouths.

They clustered around Lenith, plucking at her sleeve and touching her face with their thin, cold fingers.

"Where are we?" a woman asked. "Where are my family?"

"I'm a general." A man pushed to the front of the crowd. He'd been buried in armour. It was scuffed and faded with wear. He drew himself up in front of Lenith. She scrambled to her feet again and walked around him. "I commanded armies. I've killed kings. You have to help me."

Lenith got to her feet. She pushed through the growing crowd of ghosts. The clung to her, pressing their faces close to hers.

T.A. Moore

"What do we do?"
"Where?"
"Why?"

Lenith ignored them all. They were old dead who had never crossed the river to be sorted and judged by their gods; they were confused and unhappy things. Their memories were fragmented, clinging to the remnants of their lives and achievements. It was a waste of time to try and explain they were dead.

She knelt down beside the river. The stones dug into her knees through her jeans. She tore a strip from the bottom of her shirt. A button popped loose from the garment. It arched through the air and plopped into the water. Ripples spread out from where it landed. Lenith wadded the strip of fabric up and dipped it into the river.

The dead kept pleading with her.

"Help us?"
"We're lost."
"My husband will pay."
"My family needs me."

The dark, slow-moving river was glacial despite the oppressive heat. It felt thick, too thick to be water; almost as if she could have picked up a handful of it.

She let the rag unfurl, holding onto the end of it. The long strip of fabric unfurled, caught by the current, and rippled through the water. Lenith gathered it back up in her hands and stood up smoothly, the long muscles in her thighs tensing. Water dripped between her fingers, fat drops spattering over the ground, which drank it thirstily, as she climbed back up the hill.

The dead tried to follow her but quickly lost interest. Their minds were fragmented; their attention span shattered. Without Lenith to distract them they went back to wandering aimlessly, acting out a mummer's play of their lives.

By the she got to the top of the hill Lenith's knees were covered with mud. The cuffs of her sleeves were soaked. Dumuzi raised his head from his chest when he heard her approaching.

His jaw moved, tendons popping in his cheeks.

The Even

"Do you have the water?" he asked.

"Yes." Lenith stood on her tiptoes and pressed the damp cloth to Dumuzi's lips. He sucked at it, dampening his lips and the tarry flap of his tongue. Before he had his fill Lenith took the cloth away. "Well?"

"Water." Dumuzi demanded, stretching his neck after the dripping cloth. "I said you'd tell me if you gave me water."

Lenith nodded.

"And I gave you water," she said. "Now tell me who has passed here and you can have the rest of it."

Dumuzi moaned and went sullenly silent. Lenith waited, turning the damp cloth in her hand. He was the first to surrender.

"Many have passed in the last few days," he said reluctantly. "Many always pass. How am I meant to know who you are interested in?"

Lenith leant against the rock. She picked at a smear of mud on the back of her hand.

"Tell me about all of them," she said.

Dumuzi sighed.

"I know not the days. Nor how long passed between one and the next. Time is hard to judge here. The gnomes came; I know them by their smell and their snorting. They had a man with them. He cursed the world up one side and down the other, damning everyone in it for cowards."

"The Yekumi," Lenith said. "I cannot blame him for taking the whole thing ill."

A sigh rattled from Dumuzi's chest. "Ah, Yekum. So it was to the Even you fled, Lenith? After abandoning your post."

"I need answers," Lenith said. "Not judgement. Who else passed before you?"

Dumuzi dropped his head again, as if he was to weary to support the weight of his own skull. Hanks of dull, tangled hair hung around his cadaverous features. There were round, raw sores on the top of his skull where the birds had picked the hair away.

"A man and a woman, separately and together. They visited

often over the last long days. Others came with them but they were irrelevant. The man, the woman: they were in charge."

"Tell me of them."

"They did not stray far from the arch," Dumuzi said. "They were not of here and were not meant to be here; they were alive. Their presence roused the harpies and made the dead who keep me company... hungry. Each time they came they lingered, then were driven back to the living world. The two should not mix: the dead and the living."

"What where they like, this man and woman. What made you single them out?"

"They were obeyed. The others were just servants," Dumuzi said dismissively. "The woman was a viper, quick and deadly. Her words were like splinters, shaped to work under the skin and cause infection. Mistakes were viciously punished. One of the souls who entered with her did not leave. His bones lie to the west. The man had a golden tongue and sounded weary. He spoke of rest, and he pitied me."

"And you say they were before the gnomes carried the Yekum to their lair?" Lenith asked.

"Yes," Dumuzi said. "I could not say how many days before but the order is right. The man, the man and the woman together, the woman alone and the gnomes. I have answered your questions; I have done what you asked. Now, give me water."

Dumuzi had told her what he knew. Lenith reached up and pressed the rag to his mouth. The heat had evaporated most of the moisture in it but the god still suckled at it greedily. If it had been an emotion that she had been conceived of possessing Lenith would have felt pity for him too.

Pity, however, was

The Even

not an attribute that mortals cared about in their gods. Not in Lenith's day at least.

There was only so much moisture the rag could hold. When it was dry Lenith took it from Dumuzi and tucked it into her pocket. The end of it hung loose, flapping in the wind. She looked up at Dumuzi. The water had done little to moisten the sun-baked leather of his flesh. His head lolled tiredly.

"How long will you stay here?" she asked suddenly. "Your wife is faithless, your worshippers…" her hand fluttered dismissively in the air. "… gone. Why stay?"

"I love my wife," Dumuzi answered tiredly. "And it is my nature to be… loyal. Steadfast. Why did you leave?"

That question went unanswered. Lenith left Dumuzi there, the dead returning to cluster around his rock, and walked away.

Ten

The Deadlands were vast and interconnected. Hell and Hades, Purgatory and the Flowerlands; they were all contained within. Here the spirits of the dead and the spirits of the never-living dwelt side by side.

There was beauty. The great palaces of those who ruled here stretched towards the unchanging sky with fingers of bone and stone. Pennants, sigils stitched in gold and bright threads, flapped from the peaks of the towers. In the quiet, clean cities elegant sculptures of scraped bone and furled skin grew in the squares. In the green North vast, lush orchards of bone grey trees grew; their boughs weighed down with over-ripe, black and scarlet fruit the size of a large man's fist. To the cold South there were glittering pillars carved from ice, each containing a frozen, screaming soul.

The Even

But that was inside the borders of the black river. No one claimed the lands beyond. That was where the dead waited: those who lacked the ferryman's coin or whose fear of judgement overwhelmed their fear of the monsters that dwelt amidst the crags. Harpies nested on crags, foul and smelling of dung, and in the deserts ghuls lurked in pits and hunted the dead for their bones. There were other things as well. Things half-formed and mongrel that had no place in creation and so clung here, between life and death.

Fending off extinction.

Eleven

Dumuzi's rock had disappeared behind her. Lenith passed the greenswarded death mounds of Heitsi-eibib and crossed the flattened spoor of the Hungry Ghosts. The ground was wet with spit from their empty mouths. Harpies spun overhead, their wings shedding, spinning cruciform shadows on the ground, but they were scavengers. The confused dead were their prey, not Gods. Lenith bowed her head and walked on, long legs carrying her over the stony desert.

Her destination grew slowly closer: a black cathedral that thrust up out of the earth like an erupting tooth. From a distance it was an impressive structure, but as she got closer Lenith could see the broken down walls, cracked towers and empty windows. Whoever worshipped here had abandoned it a long time ago.

Lenith finally reached the huge, wrought iron gates. She stopped in front of them and looked up, the twisted bars painting shadows over her pale face. A chain with links as thick around as Lenith's wrist held the gates shut. Lenith put her hand on the gate and pushed gently. The chain held for a breath and then disintegrated, dust and splinters of iron falling over Lenith's desert-scarred boots. Without the chain to hold it closed the gates swung slowly open, the hinges creaking. Lenith walked through them into the cathedral's courtyard.

The marks of habitation had survived the scouring the desert winds. There were rotting baskets piled up in the corner of the courtyard. Dead, dry vines spilled out of them, forcing the wicker weave apart, and splayed over the cobblestones. Vegetables that tried to go to root and found no sustenance to grow. A pile of rusted metal and mouldering wood looked to have once been a cart and a few ragged, grey banners still hung from the walls.

There were no other signs of life.

The Even

Lenith stepped forwards and something cracked underfoot. She stepped back and bent down, picking up the bloody feather. It was identical to the one she had caught in the Even Square. She ran it through her fingers, disarranging the quills.

Almost, she corrected herself, no other sign of life.

The Yekumi had been here. She held proof of that. But where was he now? That was the question. She looked down at the worn cobbles underfoot. It was the obvious place. The Yekumi had been taken by gnomes after all: earth elementals.

All she had to do was work how to find them.

Lenith tucked the quill into her shirt. Then she walked over to the huge, wooden doors that barred the way into the cathedral. Unlike the front gates, they were locked. The lock held but the wood holding it was less enduring. Lenith kicked the door twice, tearing the lock free. It landed with a rattle on the inside of the doors.

She went inside.

As it was in the Courtyard, the evidence of habitation had been reduced to splinters of wood and rotting psalm books. Shards of brightly coloured glass covered the floor: relics of once beautiful picture windows.

The only thing that had survived intact was the altar in the middle of the room. It was a single plug of basalt with a metal brazier sitting on it, the legs buried in the stone. A huge toad-headed statue stood behind the brazier, holding a simple brass bowl over a fire that had long since guttered out.

Lenith climbed up the steps to the altar and walked over to the brazier. The desiccated remains of a rat lay in the statue's bowl, stuck to the metal with a mixture of dried blood and putrefaction. Lenith sniffed the air. The smell of rot had long-since passed. It still stank of piety. This had been a sacrifice, and one more recent than the ruins of the place would suggest.

The surface of the basalt plug was thick with gritty dust, blown in through the windows from the plains outside. Lenith scuffed it aside with her boot, revealing a polished surface and a crack that ran, in a perfect circle, around the brazier. She stamped inside the

T.A. Moore

circle. Her boot made a hollow sound on the stone.

It was a trapdoor. The brazier was the lever.

Lenith grabbed the base of the tripod, braced her feet and pulled. The stone shifted but not enough. She swore softly and tried again, twisting and pulling at the same time. She had to lift it up—the rough metal biting her hands—and out of the hole, like a cork from a bottle. The air that escaped the shaft it had covered was dank and smelt of rot and mould. Screams echoed up from far below the earth. Lenith pulled the tripod backwards, the stone door scraping over the floor.

Her shoulder hit the bowl in the statue's hands and knocked it loose. It landed on its side on the basalt, denting the bowl and knocking the dried-out rat offering free. Then it rolled to the side of the plug and tumbled over. It landed on the stone floor with a noisy clatter. One that sounded particularly loud in the hush of the cathedral.

Something cracked.

"You should not be

The Even

here," a low, grating voice said.

Lenith looked up. It was too late to avoid the huge grey fist that swung at her face. She threw up her arms to protect her face. The punch hit her forearm with pulping force and threw her backwards off the altar. She was briefly airborne, then she landed with a crash in the middle of the rotting benches. She lay on her back, winded and gasping in the stink of old wood and fresh rot. Then she rolled over and pushed herself painfully to her feet.

The toad-statue, newly-animated by the wards she had violated, walked across the platform, stone feet clicking on stone. It reached the edge of the platform and walked off, crashing awkwardly to the ground. Bits of stone flew off it on impact and cracks crazed their way over its rough, grey surface.

For a moment Lenith thought it was dead. She should have known that it wouldn't be that easy. The toad-statue rose awkwardly to its feet and turned, casting around for Lenith. One side of its head was smashed, the bulging eye and half the wide mouth reduced to powder, and the hand it raised to point at her was fingerless; the missing fingers scattered over the floor of the cathedral. Lenith stepped back and stood on one, feeling it roll underfoot.

"You are flesh," it said, the groaning voice drawn from deep inside its barrel chest. "Flesh does not belong here."

"Golem," Lenith said. She scrambled to her feet. There were splinters in the palms of her hand and her forearm felt broken. She edged sideways, kicking the wooden debris out of the way. Her gaze flickered from the creature to the altar, the shaft down, and back again. "I'm not flesh, creature. I am of the Deathlands."

The toad-statue shook its broken head to the side and balled its hands into maul-sized fists. It passed judgement on her.

"You are not stone." It lumbered towards her, moving faster than would seem possible, and swung a fist at her. Lenith jumped backwards, tripped and caught herself. The fist hit the wall instead of her. A chip flew off the already damaged knuckle and skimmed Lenith's brow, slicing open her skin. Blood ran down the smooth plane of her face and dripped from the point of her chin, leaving dark, coin-sized marks in the dust that coated her. The creature swung at her again and this time she wasn't quick enough to avoid it. The broad, stone hand caught her across the side of her head, sending her flying. She landed awkwardly on hip and hand, bruising one and skinning the other. The pain was like a black starburst inside the confines of her skull, blinding her as the blood could not. "You are not dirt. You are flesh and you. Do. Not. Belong."

The statue linked its hands together and raised them over its head, stone joints grating, and brought them down. Lenith threw herself forwards, between the creature's spread legs. She landed flat on her stomach and crawled forwards, using the flagstones as handholds. The rough edges skinned the pads off her fingers.

She rolled onto her back, curled her legs up and drove her heels into the golem's leg. It stumbled forwards and the crack in its thigh widened, sending out tributaries through its stone.

While it staggered Lenith got to her feet and made a dash for the altar. She ran up the steps, ignoring the fiery ache in her arm. The golem caught her before she reached the top of the stairs. It grabbed her ankle and pulled her feet from under her. She landed flat on her stomach, the edge of the plug digging into her stomach.

"You do not belong," it repeated.

Lenith twisted at the hips and drove her free foot into the stone-golem's already damaged face. Bits broke free from its eye and cheek, dropping to the steps with brittle, chinking noises. The golem's grip didn't loosen; things like it didn't feel pain. It dragged her down the steps, the edges digging into her hip. She lifted her leg and brought it down, hard as she could. Pain flared in the flesh of her calf, but one of the creature's fingers cracked and broke off. So Lenith did it again. The golem lost its grip on her. She scrambled to her feet, ignoring the ache in hip and leg, and hobbled back up the steps.

"You do not belong," the golem repeated.

There was a ladder in the shaft, stapled to the stone. The golem was pulling itself up onto the altar. Lenith didn't have time to be careful. She got onto the ladder, climbed down a few paces, and

The Even

kicked her feet free of the rungs. She dropped like a stone, her fingers slipping over the bars, until she grabbed hold of the ladder to stop herself. The weight of her body swinging from her hand nearly popped her shoulder out of the socket.

She cursed, taking the name of half her own pantheon in vain, and got her feet back on the rungs.

The golem leant over the shaft, blocking out the light, and groped for her with a half-fingered hand. She held her breath. It turned out she was just too low for it to touch. Just. She felt its flat, brutal fingers brush her hair..

Lenith slid down another step, making sure she was out of reach. She rested her forehead against the rung. It was rough, rusty, and cold. She only rested for a moment. The golem couldn't reach her, but it wasn't giving up either. It kept trying to reach her and each time it did, it jarred the ladder.

She looked down. The ladder disappeared down into the darkness. It seemed to go on for miles. Lenith took a deep breath and started to climb down: one rung at a time.

Twelve

Halfway down the golem lost interest in her. It moved away from the top to the shaft, a square of light appearing overhead. It was still up there, but that was a problem for later.

Lenith kept climbing. Whoever she'd heard, when first she opened the shaft, was still screaming, their voice rising and falling in a ragged rhythm. At first it was impossible to make out the words. The further down Lenith climbed, the clearer they got.

It was the Unnamed One. He begged for it to stop and threatened them with Yekumi vengeance in the same breath. The boy had front if nothing else.

The screams were almost hypnotic. It caught Lenith by surprise when she reached the bottom of the ladder. She had not looked down since she could remember. It didn't matter. There was no-one waiting for her. Either the disturbance caused by the statue wakening was not unusual, or it had been passed unnoticed below.

The screams reached a raw peak and then gurgled to a stop. Maybe they had cut out the Yekumi's tongue.

Lenith crept down the passageway, trailing her fingers along the wall, until she reached the entrance that led to the main cavern. She hid in the shadows and, despite herself, she was impressed. The cathedral on the surface was a replica, writ small and reversed, of this underground throne room.

Stalagmites formed long, glassy white columns the height of a three storey house that glowed softly to fill the cave with dim light. Stone angels, ruined wings spread as if they were trying to take flight, decorated half of the columns. It was odd choice for earth elementals. The dark grey roof and walls of the cave were threaded with strands of silver and milky ribbons of ore and gems. A huge throne stood in the middle of the cave. It had been

The Even

carved from a single giant garnet and the angled facets caught and reflected the light.

It was beautiful, but nothing could improve the figure that squatted in it. The Lord of the Realm of Earth was a grey, leathery creature with a fat body, thin limbs and flat, wide-mouthed head. He bore a great resemblance to the toads that his people were wont to disguise themselves as. His eyes were closed, slices of bilious green just visible between the warty lids, and his concave chest rose with each shallow, bubbling breath.

Around him the gnomes and goblins busied

themselves.. Some plunged their broad, spatulate fingers into the earth, seeding gems and chunks of metal and fossils. Others sat, backs hunched and bodies puffed out fatly, with their mouths placed on vents and exhaled great gouts of greenish gas.

Lenith cut her goggling short. There was still a task to complete. She looked around the cavern for the Yekumi youth. There was no sign of him. She edged out of the shadows to get a better view. A chill ran down her back at the exposure. She still couldn't see the Yekumi. Hear him, yes. He hadn't resumed his begging but he was moaning, thick, badly hurt noises. But where, Lenith shifted forward another inch and a thick twist of hair fell over her brow, was he?

Something cracked.

Lenith snapped her head around in the direction of the noise. One of the grieving marble angels had... moved. There was a crack in one of the great wings and beneath the stone there was a slice of raw, weeping flesh. While she watched he raised his head, dusty grey hair hanging over a face turned gaunt with pain. His lips were stitched together with wire and fresh and old blood drooled down his chin. Thin threads of milky stone had invaded his face, branching over his cheeks and then following the big vein down into his neck. His eyes were the worst. They were blank, oval balls of stone: like marbles.

"Ahh." Lenith sighed her realization. She counted the statues quickly. There were twelve frozen statues bound to the slender pillars. There had only been eight Yekumi sacrificed while she had been in the city: one for dallying outside the family, two for treachery and the rest... because the Yekum wanted them dead. The others must have been before her time. She had never inquired how many of the Yekumi had been dragged down into the earth. "They tether them here, encase them."

The cruelty of it was impressive. The Yekumi were creatures of the air; to be bound would be torment for them. Unfortunately, it did make Lenith's task more difficult. Instead of being chained with metal or magic the Yekumi were chained with their own flesh. Both their hands and the back of their heads had been

The Even

melded with the stone that was infecting them. And what gifts Lenith had did not grant her mastery of either stone or flesh: not living flesh.

She located her Yekumi, the one least infected by the spreading stone leprosy. He was strung up to the pillar nearest the throne. A gnome was in the middle of tying off the stitches in his lips. Fresh blood dripped from the cleft in his chin. Lenith pulled one of the canvas bags from her pocket. She picked at the knot patiently, unravelling it strand by strand, and walked into the cavern.

Her boot heels echoed loudly from the high, curved walls. On the third step the Earth King stirred and on the seventh he raised his head from his breast. Dull yellow-green eyes swept over the cavern to see who'd disturbed him. They widened when he saw Lenith, bulging, and he slapped his hand on the arm of the throne.

"I don't know you." He licked the air with a flat, black tipped tongue and twisted his wide face like he didn't like the taste. "You do not belong here."

Lenith crossed the distance to the throne. The goblins and gnomes had abandoned their tasks. They formed a rough, unfriendly circle around her, blocking her escape. She propped her free hand on her hip and cocked her head to the side.

"So I have been told," she said. "Nevertheless, here I remain."

She gave an insolent sketch of a bow, her hand not moving from her hip.

The Earth King glowered down at her. Lenith realized how wrong her initial impression of him had been. Despite his bloated body he'd looked small, but that was an effect of the great gem-throne. In reality, he was vast. He towered over her. The hand he used to scratch his stomach was twice the size of her head.

"So you are." He blinked, his eyelids not quite in synch, and leant forwards bracing his hand on his knee. Translucent webbing linked his spindly, big-knuckled fingers. "And I know you. Why do you intrude on us, Faceless?"

The bag's knot finally gave way. Lenith curled her fingers around the bag to stop it spilling its contents. A few grains slipped between her fingers. The gnomes snorted and edged forwards.

Their nostrils flared, wet and red, as they snuffled at the air. The King growled at them and they froze, but they crouched low and held the ground taken.

Lenith waited for the disruption to die down. Once the gnomes were silent she turned and pointed at the half-transformed Yekumi with her chin.

"I want him."

Silence met her demand. Then the king started to rock backwards and forwards, burping with laughter. His subjects ignored him. They were too simple creatures to have use for humour.

The King finally got control of himself.

"For love?" he asked. "For love you invade our domain, Faceless? I had thought the time for such epic quests was long past."

"I'm not here for love," Lenith said. Disdain dripped from her words. Then she paused to

The Even

rethink her answer. "Well, not my own at least."

"Then what are you here for?" The King sat back, his belly folding, and laid his hands over it. "Money? Renown?"

"Boredom, curiosity. Do my motives really matter?" She held her hands up, letting a trickle of salt and dirt fall from one hand to the other. The ring of gnomes moaned softly and edged forwards. A grinding noise from their king stilled them again. "I want the Yekumi, Earth King, and I can pay."

The King licked the air again. His hands tightened around the arms of the chair. But he had better control of himself than his subjects. He shook his head, rolling it from side to side.

"He is our prey."

Lenith spread her fingers. More mixed-dirt fell to the ground, covering the toes of her boots. She tightened her fingers, stopping the flow, and the gnomes all groaned wetly. The King lowered warty lids over his bulbous eyes.

"If he's your prey," Lenith said, "you can do what you like with him."

The salt-seasoned ground was too much of a temptation. First one gnome broke rank, dashing forwards to lick the ground, and then the others followed. They shoved and shouldered each other; their tongues sandpapered with grit and salt. Lenith tightened her fingers around the bag and stepped away from them. She divided her attention between them and the King.

His attention was on his feeding subjects.

"We are bound…" His voice trailed off and he shook his head. "We are bound to take those of his name when we find them."

Lenith leant forwards. She dropped her voice.

"But are you bound to keep them?"

The Earth King turned his head and spat a tarry lump onto the ground.

"We keep them here because we hate them. Things of the air that they are," he spat again to clear his throat. "All we are bound to is to bring them here, once they are here they cannot leave. The gates of Death only open one way."

"Except for the likes of us."

T.A. Moore

The Earth King gestured back over his shoulder at the frozen statues. The Yekumi screamed behind the stitched gag and struggled against the stone that shackled him. His lean, grey and white body formed a tight, quivering arch until his bones creaked audibly.

"Leave him here; at least he will be with his kin," the King said. "He is not of the Deadlands. Even if we gave him up, which we are loathe to do, he cannot return to the City. So what's the point?"

Lenith shrugged back at the King, an expressive roll of her shoulders. She held up her hand, the open-mouthed bag resting in the cup of her palm. The King's mouth dropped open greedily.

"I could ask you the same question." Lenith said. "If he cannot leave then why thwart me? His pain doesn't feed you, his form doesn't please you...." she let her voice trail off and closed her fingers around the bag, hiding it from sight. "Give him to me. I'm willing to pay, salt and dirt, and, if you're right, he will still be trapped this side of the gate."

The Earth-King's throat pulsed, in and out, and he ran his fingers down his stomach as he stared at her.

"I think you are trying to trick me, Faceless," he said, leaning forwards. "Perhaps I should take the payment and bind you to a pillar. Add to our collection."

"You could try," Lenith corrected and waited.

The King stared at her, expecting her to threaten or bargain with him. When she didn't he grunted and flopped back into his throne.

"Arrogant," he said.

"Perhaps," Lenith said easily. She stood hip-shot and at ease. "I am diminished but I am still a god of this place, Elemental. Do you really think you are powerful enough to bind me here against my will?"

The Earth King surged to his feet. He lumbered down the steps of the throne towards Lenith. His shadow engulfed her. The gnomes scattered, hurrying back to their neglected duties.

Lenith lifted her blank face to him and laughed.

The Even

It was a cold, clear sound, full of the essence of the Deathlands. The elemental hesitated. He was a power, here, but once he had been just another belching, snuffling gnome. Lenith had never been other than what she was.

The Earth King joined in with Lenith's laughter. He waved one big, flipper-like hand with casual magnanimity.

"I think you are a fool, Faceless. But if you want to pay to give the Yekumi a greater run of the Deathlands, who am I to thwart you?" He held his cupped hands out. "Pay me, Faceless, and you'll have your pet Yekumi."

Lenith made a dry sound and shook her head.

"Release him," she said. "And I'll pay you."

The Earth King grunted in disappointment but didn't seem surprised at the condition. He waddled over to the pillar. The touch of flat, webbed fingers turned the milky stone to a pliable, semi-liquid. He drew the Demon-kin's limbs free, one at a time.

While he was preoccupied with that Lenith pulled one of the other pouches out of her pockets. She fumbled with the knot, swearing as she tore her nail down to the quick, and filled her hands with their contents. Lenith closed her hands around the gritty mixture to stop it spilling.

The Earth-King turned, with the Yekumi youth dangling from his hand. The youth was all long bone and sparse flesh. The stumps of his ruined wings jutted from his shoulder blades. He had the flawless

73

white skin of his kin but it was pocked with rippled striates of stone and marble. The blood that dripped from his wounds was half liquid, half dust.

The Earth King opened his hand contemptuously, letting the Yekumi crumple to the ground.

"Here," he said. "Take him."

Lenith stepped forwards. She reached out to help him, until she remembered what she held in her hands. Instead of offering him a hand up she dropped to her knees beside him, tucking a shoulder until his arm.

He groaned and clutched at her shoulders, dragging her down instead of letting her help him up. His ruined wings twitched and spasmed, shedding feathers. Salt and dirt dribbled from her hands.

The Earth King watched her struggle with a certain glee.

"Well, Faceless," he said. "My payment? Or you will take his place on the pillar?"

"Stand up," Lenith hissed at the Yekumi. "Or I will give you back to them."

The Yekumi moaned at the threat, his breath hot against Lenith's neck, and pulled himself up, using her as a ladder. His knees nearly buckled under his weight but he stiffened them and raised his chin. The arrogance bred into his blood and bone could be seen in the set of his shoulders, the jut of his jaw. It was the only thing keeping him upright.

"Faceless..." The Earth King held out his hands again. They trembled slightly with greed. "My payment."

Lenith held her closed fists over the Elemental's waiting hands. A few grains fell from her fingertips to bounce against his palms. His fingers twitched and curled in anticipation. Lenith watched him. Then she threw her arms to the side and opened her fingers, spraying the salt and dirt across the cavern. It was too much temptation for the gnomes. They fell on the scattered bounty, licking the ground and fighting each other for a taste. The Earth King threw his head back and screamed in rage, his throat swelling.

The Even

The Yekumi watched with glazed, uncomprehending eyes.

"Move," Lenith snapped. She gave him a push to get him moving. He stumbled into a loose-limbed walk. Lenith pushed him again. "Run, Yekumi."

He groaned but obeyed, forcing himself into a shuffling lope. They ran through the cavern, dodging around and stepping over the feeding gnomes. The Yekumi had to duck his head and pull his shoulders in to fit through the low, narrow doorway. His wings still scraped the stone, leaving bloody trails high on the wall. He stopped at the base of the ladder and plucked at the wire in his lips.

Lenith grabbed his hands and pulled them down.

"We don't have time. Keep moving." She cocked her head to the side, listening. The tumult in the cavern was dying down "The salt won't hold them for long."

The Yekumi baulked, shaking his head. His fingers plucked clumsily at the thin wire stitches that dug into his lips. Lenith grabbed his wrists, her hands not close to spanning them, and glared at him.

"If they catch you," she said, "the stitches will be the least of your worries."

The Earth-King roared again, shaking dust from the ceiling. It made the Yekumi wince. He nodded his agreement to Lenith, dipping his chin twice, and she moved his hands to the ladder.

"Then climb," she told him.

His fingers flexed, making the rusted metal creak, and he started to climb. It was still a tight fit. He had to keep shoulders and wings hunched in to his body. Spasms made the heavy muscles in his back jump and twitch under the white and marble skin. Despite that he kept climbing, speeding up his steps the closer he got to the square of light at the top of the tunnel.

Lenith scrambled up behind him. She was grimly aware that they were climbing too slow.

Thirteen

They got halfway up the shaft before the Earth King sent his subjects after them. The gnomes came racing up after them; some climbed the ladder, claws scraping rusted flakes from the metal, while others crawled straight up the wall.

After one look down Lenith ignored them. She concentrated on climbing, one hand over the other. It wasn't until they clawed at the heels of her boots that she paid them any heed. She kicked down at them, driving her heel into their faces. They slipped from the ladder and fell, flailing and twisting, until they hit the bottom of the shaft. Then they scrambled back to their

The Even

feet, shook themselves off and started to climb again.

Earth elementals were, by their nature, sturdy.

Lenith pulled the last pouch from her pocket. She didn't have time to open it, so she just tossed it down into the rising tide of elementals. They tore it to shreds, showering themselves in salt, and fought bloodily over the scraps of cloth. While they fought, chewing and biting each other to get every last grain, Lenith and the Yekumi finished their climb.

The Yekumi reached the top first. Lenith hooked one arm around the ladder and waited, keeping an eye on the brawling gnomes. The minute he was out she followed him, scrambling out in a graceless sprawl of long, lanky limbs. She grabbed the brazier and pulled it towards the hole. The Yekumi took it off her and lifted it easily. He drove it down and twisted, screwing it in securely.

Lenith left him to it and looked around for the stone-golem. It stood in the aisle, between the pews, and stared blankly at her with its one eye. It showed no sign of moving. Whatever enchantment brought it to life obviously didn't include stopping people leave the caverns.

There was a wet, ripping noise from behind her. Lenith turned. The Yekumi had picked the stitches free from his lips. The wire hung in a loose spiral from his hand. Blood dribbled down his chin from the holes in his lips. He worked his mouth until he got his tongue working again.

"Di...did the Yekum send you?" he asked. "W...who....who else is here?"

Lenith pushed her hair back from her face, tucking the dreads behind her ears. The Yekumi's eyes barely flickered over the blank skin where her face should be. Of course, she supposed he had seen worse things: here and in the Yekum's Palace.

"All the dead in the world, every last one. If you mean who else was sent..." She let her voice trail off and sketched a mocking bow. "There's just me. And I do not think the Yekum sent me, Nameless."

The Yekumi bristled at her. His chin lifted and he looked down his nose at her. He must be feeling better if he could muster arrogance.

"I have a name," he said. "I am, my name is...is..."

His mouth worked soundlessly around the word that he was trying to remember. He couldn't quite force it over his tongue.

Lenith watched him struggle for a moment. Then she shook her head.

"Your name was stricken from the walls," she said. "You are Nameless, you are Dust."

He glared at her, coin-gold eyes sullen under straight brows.

"I am Yekumi."

They didn't have time for this. Lenith wiped her muddy hands down her legs.

"You were Yekumi. Now you are dust. Nameless" She poked her finger against the rune marked in ash on his chest. "Aphar."

A shudder ran through the demon-kin's battered body. Then his lips pressed into a thin line and he tossed his head, pale hair flying around his face.

"Then that will be my name. I am Aphar, woman. Not Nameless."

Lenith shrugged. It didn't matter to her what he called himself.

"Very well," she said. "You are Aphar."

The acknowledgement of his new name took the steel from Aphar's back. Without

The Even

anger to bolster them his knees gave way beneath him. He sat down on the cold stone and pressed his hand to his forehead. Lenith noticed that the marks of torture had already started to fade from his skin. But instead of fresh skin there were scars of stone striating his skin and cupping the arch of his ribs. Only the stumps of his wing were not healing.

He was still beautiful. They might have stripped the Yekumi name from him but they couldn't take their radiant heritage from his blood. Slender and blonde, his pale skin stippled with paler, glossy scars, he gleamed in the dim light.

"We should go," Lenith said. "Once the Earth King composes himself he will send his people after us."

She jumped off the altar and walked towards the hall, keeping a wary eye on the Golem as she stepped around it. It didn't so much as twist. She was halfway to the door when the Yekumi called her back.

"Wait," he said. "You were sent for me; you cannot abandon me here."

Lenith turned around. The Yekumi stood at the edge of the altar, his stumps spread in an attempt to remind her of his authority. Instead, it simply reminded her what he had lost. What had been taken from him.

"I said we," she pointed out. "Now hurry up. We need to get out of their lands."

Golden eyes looked away from her. The mask of his inbred arrogance shattered and fear crawled up through the cracks.

"I cannot." He stepped back from the altar. The ragged white kilt that was his only garb fluttered around his thighs. "I am Yekumi, we do not walk on the earth. That is our curse."

Lenith turned and walked to the door. She pushed it open. A harpy had settled in the courtyard to eat its prey. It screeched and took off, flapping furiously, at the disturbance. The remains it had been feasting on fell from its claws. The remains of the soul-flesh, an arm and part of a chest, lay on the ground. Then, without the memory of the spirit to hold it together, it faded to nothing.

"You aren't Yekumi anymore." She half-turned, framed in the

stone arch. "I don't think the curse will have any power over you."

The Yekumi lifted his chin. He took a deep breath, his nostrils flaring.

"Think?"

Lenith shifted her weight. She was eager to go before the Earth King sent his gnomes after them. The altar itself was impervious to them, basalt had too much fire in its making for them to have an affinity to it, but the ground she stood on was not so protected.

"You cannot fly and I am not going to carry you," she said. "So either you walk or you stay here and wait for the Earth King to come and get you."

Aphar looked down at the dirt with a sick expression on his face.

"What if you're wrong?"

"Then you get dragged back down and chained back to that pillar, just like the rest of your kin. But stay there and the same thing will happen. It's your choice."

Lenith left the Cathedral and walked across the courtyard, crushing harpy feathers underfoot. She reached the walls before she heard the Yekumi, no, Aphar, behind her. With his long legs it didn't take him long to catch up with her. He fell in beside her as she walked through the gates. Since he hadn't been dragged underground, not yet, anyhow, it seemed she'd been right about the curse. Not that he acknowledged that with so much as a tilt of his head.

They walked in silence, alongside her earlier tracks, leaving them undisturbed on a whim. A dark ferry drifted by but the hooded boatman showed no interest in them. His fares were plentiful enough. He had no need to tout for trade. On the crest of a nearby hill a flock of Ciuteoteos rattled their spears and flashed painted, naked limbs aggressively.

It was what occurred behind them that concerned Lenith, but she didn't look back. They would know when the gnomes were on them — constantly looking over their shoulders would just slow them down.

The Even

It was Aphar who broke the silence, stretching his legs to fall into step beside her.

"You said the Yekumi didn't send you."

Lenith shook her head. "I did not."

Aphar gave her a black, impatient look. He stopped and grabbed her shoulder, jerking her around to face him. His fingers dug into her flesh, seeking bone.

"Do not try to be clever with me, woman," he said. "You said that the Yekumi had not sent you to rescue me."

Lenith put her hand on his chest. Where there was flesh it was warm, but the bands of invasive stone were cold. She pushed him away from her, making him snarl.

"I said I did not know who sent me to retrieve you, Aphar. Oeillet's Tallyman acted as an intermediary for my employer. They did not think I needed to know more than the task in hand. I do not think it was the Yekumi; he is mercurial but even he is unlikely to sentence you to death and then beg for your return the same day. Once we return to the city you will find out who it was." She turned and walked away. "Then you can decide if this was a rescue or not."

This time Aphar didn't follow her. She stopped and looked back. He stood where she had left him, his hands curled into big, stone knuckled fists.

"You do not know?" he said. "What if they are my enemy; what if they mean me harm?"

"That isn't my problem," Lenith said.

Aphar stared at her, his mouth twisting into a sneer.

"I have no liking for you." he said.

"Surprisingly, you are not the only one," Lenith said. The earth rolled under her feet, making her stagger. She caught herself and looked back towards the Black Cathedral. The walls had tumbled out and the ground had cracked open. Sulphurous gas poured from the chasm, blighting the earth where it spread. "The Earth King, for one, shares your view."

The gnomes crawled out of the sulphur cloud, crawling over and under each other into the hurry. There were hundreds of them. They turned flat, pug-nosed faces, sniffing the air, until they caught their prey's scent. Then they ran, staying low to the ground and using all four limbs.

Lenith swore flatly and ran. There was no point in trying to hide. Even if they could find a hiding place in the flat, barren plains, the gnomes would still scent them out. Aphar kept pace with her easily. He tossed quick, sporadic looks over his shoulder.

"They're catching up," he reported.

Lenith grunted and pushed herself to run faster. Even though she was aware it wasn't fast enough to make a difference.

"Where are we going?" Aphar asked. Lenith gave him a suspicious, side-long look. He pressed for an answer. "Where?"

"To the gateway near Kur where Dumuzi hangs," Lenith said finally. When Aphar growled his incomprehension she gestured towards the slow-flowing river. "Follow the River till you find the dull red rock where a god hangs from a rock. The gateway is there."

Aphar nodded. He ran alongside her in silence. This time it was Lenith who risked a look over her shoulder. The gnomes crested the hill behind them, running in silence.

"Can you do it?" Aphar asked. "No weaselling words or mockery, just tell me the truth. Can you get me back to the City?"

"Yes."

Aphar clenched his jaw and nodded. Then he picked Lenith up, swinging her thin form up into his arms easily. She swore and struggled, twisting like an eel. He just tightened his arms around her and sped up. His long legs ate up the scorched, rocky ground and his inhuman strength kept them just ahead of the gnomes, although the creatures still dogged their heels.

Fourteen

They reached Kur minutes ahead of the gnomes. For the last few miles they had left a trail of blood behind them. There were no calluses on Aphar's feet; like all his kind he had walked rarely and never been hunted. The stony ground had blistered and torn his feet.

Aphar stopped in front of Dumuzi's rock and lowered Lenith to the ground. He studied the swinging ruin of the god's gaunt and desiccated body.

"This is what you call a god?" he asked sceptically. "This crow-bait?"

Lenith tugged her jacket straight and patted her pockets, checking that everything was still in place.

"It doesn't matter what I call him. He is a god." She looked back towards their pursuers. Then she turned her attention to Aphar when he muttered in disbelief. "Do not look so surprised, Aphar. You were not in much better condition when you were a guest in the Earth King's Palace."

Aphar curled his lip, "I was not dead."

"Nor am I," Dumuzi said. He raised his head and swung it blindly towards Aphar. "He is what you came for, Lenith the Faceless? Some demon child the gnomes had stolen away?"

Aphar scowled. "I am no child," he said sullenly.

"Yes, he is," Lenith said. Although she wasn't contradicting Aphar he turned his scowl on her. She ignored him and checked her pockets again. They had to be here. She'd had them earlier.

"Why did you bother?" Dumuzi mocked her. "Once they are here, the living cannot leave again. For them, the doorway only swings one way."

Aphar struck Dumuzi across the face, setting the god to swinging.

"You lie. She said she could take me back to the city."

Dumuzi swung on the hook, wheezing with laughter. "She lied! She lied to you, demon," he crowed. "She lied, and now the gnomes will rip you to pieces. That will be your eternity, your punishment for trusting a faithless god."

Aphar raised his hand again. Instead of hitting Dumuzi around he spun around and stared at Lenith accusingly.

"Does he speak the truth?" he asked raggedly. "Did you lie to me? Are we trapped here?"

Lenith's fingertips brushed the smooth, porous curve of knucklebone in the bottom of her pocket. She wrapped her fingers around it so tightly it made her hand ache.

"Don't be a fool," she said. "In case you haven't noticed, I did not endear myself to the elementals. They are chasing me too. If I didn't think I could get you back to the City, I wouldn't have come here."

Aphar stared at her. "If you're lying to me..." he threatened softly.

"What? You'll spit at me when we're both chained to the Earth King's pillars?" She held her hand out, the stewed knucklebones lying on her palm. "Swallow these."

Aphar picked the bones up, between finger and thumb. He eyed them sceptically.

"Bones?"

"Just swallow them," Lenith said.

Aphar grimaced. He popped the bones in his mouth, closed his eyes and swallowed hard. They caught in his throat and he coughed, gulped and rubbed his chest.

"And now?" he asked.

Lenith headed towards the misty boundary. "Follow me," she said. "We'll be back under the Even soon."

Dumuzi wailed, furious and bereft, behind them.

"She lied to you, boy! She lied...we're all trapped here! All of us," his voice echoed back at him from the empty wasteland. "Trapped."

Fifteen

The cool fingers of mist tugged at Lenith's hair and fingers, trying to pull her back. She shook her head, pulled her fingers free and walked on. There was nothing to go back to. Only empty tasks and her despondent sisters.

Aphar followed close on her heels. Every few steps his hand sought out her shoulder, checking that she was still there. With nothing else to distract her she found herself wondering about her companion again. Who had wanted him back to the City so badly, and why?

"Where are we going?" Aphar asked.

"The City," Lenith answered, stepping over a rut in the dirt. "Where else?"

"No. Where are we going once we get there?" he asked.

Lenith turned slightly to the left, moving against the tug of the internal compass that led her home.

"I will give you over to the Tallyman," she said. "What happens after that is up to them."

"You don't even know why they want me," Aphar said.

"No."

"Whatever they offered you," Aphar said. "I have friends in the City who will match it. They will buy my freedom. You cannot just sell me to this Tallyman."

Lenith laughed. The mist did nothing to deaden the sound.

"You jest," she said. "Everything, and everyone, is for sale in Even City. You are Yekumi, you should know that better than anyone else. As for your friends, I doubt they would part with a clipped stater for you now. The Yekum himself sentenced you to death as a traitor and had your name struck from the Wall. That severs all bonds of obligation, including friendship. The Tallyman's Master is the only one who wants you, Aphar. You should be glad of that. Whatever she wants you for, there is a good chance it is better than serving as a decoration in the Earth-King's palace for eternity."

There was no answer from Aphar to that. Lenith walked on, until she realized that Aphar wasn't behind her. She turned but he was gone, vanished into the mist.

"Nameless," she yelled. "Aphar."

He didn't answer. With a sigh Lenith turned and walked back the way she came. She followed the smell of burnt apples, the scent of his essence, until she found him. He was walking through the mist, back the way they'd come. More or less.

"What are you doing," Lenith asked.

He gave a furious, frightened look over his shoulder. Ragged hanks of silver blonde hair hung over his sharp, sculpted features and his golden eyes glowed in the dim light.

"Going back. What is there for me in the City now. I am outcaste, nameless. A slave bought for a handful of stater."

"More than a handful," Lenith corrected him. "The Tallyman has taken on my debt. To pay that off, you would need a houseful of stater."

It was Aphar's turn to laugh, a strained, ragged sound with no joy in it. He flung his arm out and started walking again.

"Is that meant to comfort me?" he asked.

Lenith sped her pace and stepped in front of him, blocking his path. He could have stepped around her easily, there were no marked routes in the mist, but he stopped.

"I am not a creature for comfort," she said.

Aphar gave her a scathing look from head to booted toe and every bony inch between. His lip curled in a sneer.

"I can see that," he said.

"What point is there in going back?" she asked, ignoring the insult. "If you remain the Earth King will not rest until you are chained to his pillar again. You don't know what your fate will be if you return to the City. There is always a chance that the Tallyman's Master won't want you for anything that you would deem repugnant. Perhaps I was wrong and she is one of those friends of yours."

Aphar shook his head.

"Might and perhaps aren't good enough reasons to go back," he said. "I would rather take my chances in the Deathlands, than have everyone in the City see me fallen and paraded like a monkey on a leash."

"Do you really think any of them care?" Lenith asked. "Or that they even knew your name back when it could be spoken?"

A muscle jumped in Aphar's cheek at the jibe but he didn't move. Lenith slashed her hand through the air impatiently.

"You can't say here," she said.

"Why not," he asked.

"Because it is foolish. You do not even know your way back to the Deathlands. The gate at Kur is the only way back for you; one wrong step, one turn in the wrong direction and you would never find your way out of this mist."

The corner of Aphar's mouth twitched into a wicked, sour smile.

"Surely," he said. "That's not your problem."

Arrogant fool. He thought he could comport himself as he was still a Yekumi, the elite son of the Palace.

"Then stay here," Lenith said. "See what joy that brings you."

She went to walk away but Aphar's voice summoned her back.

"You can't leave me." Despite his arrogance he couldn't quite manage to sound sure of himself. "They paid you to bring me back. If they go back empty-handed, people will be displeased."

"So? We have already discussed the fact that people often do not warm to me. The Tallyman and his mistress would be just two more to add to the list."

"They wouldn't pay your debts off. You would be indebted to Oelliet as deeply as ever."

Lenith shrugged and spread her hands. The mist thickened around her hands, exploring the webbing between her fingers and the mounds of her thumbs, until it looked like she held a palmful of it.

"What do you want," she asked. "We cannot remain here and I

will not return to the Deathlands."

In the distance something howled. Other howls answered it. The mist deadened the sounds, flattened them. They could have come from anywhere, near or far.

"There are reasons to go back to the city: vengeance, love, hate," Lenith said. The hounds belled again. Despite the mist Lenith thought they sounded closer. She pointed up. "And there's one good reason to leave."

Aphar turned, scanning the mist to try and pinpoint the sound. The Hunt belled again and he grimaced. When he still didn't move Lenith shrugged and turned her back on him. He grabbed her arm, his fingers easily cuffing her bicep.

"I am no traitor," he said.

"So?" Lenith pried his fingers off her arm. The expression of bafflement on his face made her laugh. The mist thickened around her. Ghostly regalia clung to her shoulders and framed her face. She shook it away, her dreads whisking through the mist. "Politics might be the lifeblood of the Palace, Aphar, but to the rest of the City it's just entertainment."

Aphar grimaced and looked away from her.

"So was my death," he said in a distant voice. "I remember, they just watched me get pulled down into the earth. The Tallymen were there. While I waited for the sentence to be carried out I saw the Tallymen there. They took bets."

He looked bereft, almost raw, at the memory. Perhaps the Yekumi really believed they were beloved, respected. Or they just did not understand the society of the City they ruled, where nothing was too sacred to lay odds on or sell.

"Are you coming or not?" Lenith asked.

Aphar blinked and looked at her again. After a moment he twisted his mouth like he tasted something sour.

"I suppose I have no choice," he muttered.

They started walking again. Lenith set a faster pace this time in the hope of avoiding drawing the attention of the Hunt. With any luck it was tracking other prey.

A Hound appeared out of the fog. It paced them through the

The Even

fog. Twisted muscles bunched and rippled under its naked skin. It had blue, human eyes. After about a quarter of a mile it peeled away and disappeared.

Lenith watched it go. They had been silent since Aphar had abandoned his brief rebellion. She realized she had been wrong about something.

"You said you weren't a treacher," she said.

Aphar gave her a surprised look. "I'm not," he said carefully. "I thought you didn't—"

"I changed my mind. The Heralds said you had been caught plotting against the Yekum himself. The City assumed it some internecine war of the family that had gotten out of hand."

There was bitterness in Aphar's voice when he answered her.

"If it was then I was not informed of it," Aphar said. "The evidence against me was false. Someone else committed the crime and made sure I would pay the price for it."

"Who?" Lenith asked.

He glanced at her and then down at his feet, watching his step.

"I don't know," he said finally.

Lenith slowed her stride and studied Aphar with interest.

"You're lying," she said.

Aphar looked up and smiled. It would have been an angelic expression, suitable for his bloodline if not for the fangs that showed behind his lips.

"I'm demon-kin," he reminded her. "And I don't like, or trust, you. My suspicions are the only power I have left. I will not surrender it just to sate your curiosity."

Lenith accepted that with a shrug. It was not an unwise decision on Aphar's part. She turned over the new information in her mind. If Aphar's story was true then the question of who hired her had been joined by the question of who implicated Aphar in treason. Or, she mused, if they were the same person.

It was interesting. She absently twisted one of her dreads. It might yet even turn out to be exciting.

Between one step and the next she felt the essence of the place change. She touched Aphar's arm to catch his attention.

"We're nearly there," she said.

Aphar searched for a door or a gateway. There was nothing like that visible. Just the same featureless grey mists that had surrounded them since they left the Deathlands.

"Are you sure?"

"Yes," Lenith said. The answer didn't satisfy Aphar. His frown made Lenith try to explain further. "It's not a place, exactly. It's a weak place in the Between and I can sense what is on the other side: the living."

"Yet I cannot?" Aphar said, still frowning.

Lenith shrugged.

"You are a demon but not of the dead. You should know well enough there is a difference."

Aphar looked sour at the reminder but he shed the mood with a toss of his head.

"What do we do when we get there?" he asked.

Lenith paused and concentrated on the sense of life she was following. She turned to the east, corrected a few degrees and tossed over her shoulder.

"You'll do what I tell you," she said.

Aphar snarled

"You're arrogant for a poverty-stricken mercenary with little visible cause for their pride," he said. "If we were in the City—"

"You'd be a nameless outcaste," Lenith reminded him. "Be more careful of your threats in future. You don't have the power to waste on empty threats. And if you want to get back the City, ever again, you'll do what you're told."

She waited until Aphar nodded. Once she was sure that the demon would heed her Lenith headed for the Gateway. She was almost on top of it before it coalesced from the mist. The general shape of it was the same on this side but instead of pitted stone it was made of glossy, white marble. Two snow-white statues, the same that Lenith had passed in the graveyard, stood on guard beside the gate.

The goat-angel blinked and pointed its muzzle at her.

"Faceless Lenith. Guardian of the Gateway," it said.

The Even

The hoofed angel took over.

"You wish passage back to the Living Shore?"

"I do," Lenith stood in front of the gate, her arms loose at her sides. "Do you have reason to stop me?"

It was the goat-angel's turn to speak.

"No." It lifted its sword, "But he must stay. He does not have right of passage, nor has any deal been brokered for his return.

Lenith stepped in front of the sword. The edged stone point dimpled her t-shirt. She lent forwards and it pierced the thin cotton and dug into the skin beneath.

"You won't let him pass?"

"The rules are set, the way is blocked," the hoofed angel said.

The goat-angel shook its head. The carefully crafted locks of hair that hung down behind its ears didn't shift.

Lenith gripped the sword. The edges dug into her hand, slicing open fingers and palm. Blood welled up between her fingers and dripped onto the ground. She gestured for Aphar to pass with her free hand.

He baulked.

"They said we couldn't pass," he pointed out.

"They said you could not pass," Lenith corrected. "Now, if you want to get back to the City, go."

She tightened her grip on the sword and impaled herself on it. The blade scraped through her breastbone, grating audibly, and caught. She made a rough, hurt sound despite herself and pulled herself forwards. The blade emerged from her back, covered with gore.

The goat-angel, its face still impassive, tried to pull the sword free. Lenith held onto the blade and wouldn't let him. It turned, dragging her in wide, staggering circles. She clung to the sword stubbornly. The hoofed angel stepped forwards, weapon raised to intervene, but hesitated to strike. Lenith was not forbidden passage, but the other angel had already struck. The conflict slowed and confused it.

Lenith lost her footing and tripped, dragging the blade down with her. She swore and yelled at Aphar, "Go."

Aphar jumped and leapt towards the gateway. The hoofed angel, sure of his duty regarding the demon at least, turned to block his way. It swung its sword and clipped Aphar's shoulder, breaking the scabbed crust from the stump of his wing. Aphar cried out in pain but didn't let it stop him. He flung himself through the gate and onto the living shore.

Once Aphar was gone Lenith stopped struggling with the goat-angel. It yanked its sword free. Lenith moaned and pressed her hand to her chest, doubling over the pain that took her breath away. Immortal or not, it was an unpleasant sensation.

The angels resumed their places by the door. Her blood dripped down the goat-angel's sword and coated its fingers.

Lenith forced herself to stand up. Her own hand was coated in blood where she pressed it against her chest.

"Can I still pass?" she asked.

Both angels bent their heads at the same time, resting their chins on their breasts. It was a sorrowful pose, for their failure.

"You are free to pass. Our brothers will retrieve your companion," one said. With their heads bent it was hard to tell which one spoke.

Lenith clenched her pale fingers in her t-shirt.

"Not my concern," she said. "I was hired to retrieve him, not keep him."

The two statues continued their mute penitence. They didn't say anything in answer to her statement. It wasn't in their purview.

With her hand still pressed to her breast Lenith essayed a sardonic bow. It took an effort of will to force herself upright again. Neither statue acknowledged her.

She walked through the Gate.

Sixteen

On the other side of the Gateway the statues' dull grey twins roamed the graveyard. Their heavy feet flattened the grass and crushed the carefully built little altars in front of the graves. Shattered pots and fluttering ribbons showed where they'd been.

Aphar crouched in the shadows of the mausoleum. He looked around at Lenith.

"They can't see me," Aphar said.

Lenith picked the clinging bits of mist from her hair and clothes. She shook them off her fingers. Away from the Between they faded into nothing. Aphar got up carefully and, keeping an eye on the statues, joined her.

"Why can't they see me?" he asked.

"Remember the bone I asked you to swallow?"

Aphar frowned and nodded.

"Yes."

"It's from a human infant," Lenith explained. "One unbaptised, unshrived. It will confuse them as long as it is in your body."

"Human?" Aphar curled his lip in distaste. He probed at his stomach, as if he could find the invasive bone under the muscle. "You put human bones inside of me?"

"It worked didn't it?" Lenith said. "Don't complain."

He made a discontented sound but stopped probing his gut.

She pulled her sodden shirt away from her chest. It made a wet, sucking sound. She poked her fingers into the hole between her breasts. It hurt, but it was already healing. She wiped her fingers on her jeans.

Aphar touched her side and drew his fingers back covered with her blood. He licked them clean.

"Old blood," he said, sucking the last drop from his finger.

T.A. Moore

Across the graveyard the hoofed angel jabbed its trident at a squealing ghoul. The gaunt, grey-skinned creature squalled and writhed, clawing up divots of grass with clawed fingers. After poking it a couple of times the angel lost interest.

It left the graveyard, followed closely by its brother. Their feet clattered and echoed against the cobblestones.

Lenith watched them go with a frown. Even in the City two angry stone angels would draw attention. People would know something had disturbed them. The people who hired her would know she'd returned.

"Tell me something, woman," Aphar said. "You've freed me from the gnomes' torture and you've brought me back to my City, making sure that no one can find me. What need do I have of you now?"

He stood too close behind her and put his hands on either side of her neck. Lenith thought about jabbing her elbow into his ribs, but it would hurt

The Even

if she hit bone.

"You mean, why shouldn't you snap my neck and disappear into the City?" she asked.

His thumbs pressed against the back of her skull. He pressed just hard enough to make it hurt.

"That is what I meant," he said.

"I'm a god," Lenith said. "A broken neck won't kill me anymore than a sword through the chest will. As for you, run if you want. Where do you think you'll go? An outcaste Yekumi who has been Unnamed, Unmade. Do you really think you will find any shelter in the city?"

His hands tightened and then he let go. Lenith turned around. Aphar had slumped back against the wall of the mausoleum.

"I really don't have any choices, do I?" he asked.

Lenith shook her head. "Not many."

He nodded. "So what now?"

"You can stay at my house until I contact the Tallyman," Lenith said. "Then they'll arrange for me to meet with whoever it is that wanted you back so badly."

"And you'll sell me to them?"

Lenith nodded. "That's right. Now, come on. We should go."

For a moment it looked like Aphar would try and thwart her. Then he sighed, shifting his ruined wings, and pushed himself off the mausoleum. Rather than taking the same gate as the statues Lenith headed for the gate on the other side of the cemetery. The only person who saw them was a half-faced hunchback. He, from the oozing sack and bloody spade he carried, was unlikely to talk overmuch about the sights he'd seen.

The wrought-iron gates in the South wall were unlocked. Lenith pushed them open, the hinges creaking, and gestured for Aphar to go first. He walked through and stopped on the other side.

"Home." He breathed in deeply and closed his eyes. A

muscle in the side of his jaw twitched nervously under his skin. "I won't be leaving again."

Lenith followed him out and pulled the gates closed behind her. She gave them a tug to make sure the latch clicked into place.

"Are you in the habit of throwing down challenges to fate?" she asked. "In your straitened circumstances you should learn that's not wise."

He shook his head. "It wasn't a challenge," he said. "Just a statement."

Lenith shrugged. If Aphar wanted to tempt ill-luck it wasn't her business. She started down the street.

This quarter of the city was a blend of futuristic and alien architecture. Glazed white spires that looked like they were made out of spun sugar stretched skywards. Glassy, round modules studded the towers. The usual inhabitants of the city were supplemented with blank-eyed, dead-faced humans with mouthless, ivory-shelled creatures attached to their spines. A new race, created by the City. Sometimes they disappeared when the streets re-arranged themselves. Other times a few of them would survive. It depended on the City's whim.

Everyone, Lenith noticed, was staring at Aphar.

"We need to get you clothes." She checked her pockets for change, emptying out the remnants of salt and dirt. There were a few tiny bronze stater in her pockets. It wasn't much. "A robe or cloak."

"A cloak? I am Yekumi," Aphar said. Lenith waited and he corrected his statement. "I was. We are the most beautiful of the demon-kin. Why should I have to cover myself?"

"To avoid drawing attention," Lenith said. She stopped at a crossroads. To the north and south were the spun-sugar confections of the spine-creatures. The streets to the east and west had more familiar buildings: brick and cobbles, wooden shutters and sullen faces. Lenith turned to the East, down Voynich Avenue. "I would prefer to keep your benefactor—"

"Purchaser," Aphar hissed the correction.

Lenith accepted it with a dismissive twitch of her shoulders.

The Even

"Whatever you judge them. I would rather have them find out that you are back when I choose, not when someone gossips about you in a pub."

"If you want to avoid drawing attention," Aphar said. "Wipe your face. It's covered with blood."

Lenith touched her face with her fingertips. There were sticky patches of gore drying on her face.

"Thanks." She pulled her sleeve down over her hand and scrubbed her face. A grogoch with thickly matted fur pushed a nightsoil cart down the street. He gave Lenith a curious look. Then he saw Aphar over her shoulder. His eyes widened and he hurried away with his shoulders hunched up to his ears. The wheels of the cart juddered over the cobbles, clots of dirt spilling off the cart. Lenith watched him disappear around the corner. She shook her head. "Although I think it's too late to try and avoid attracting notice."

Aphar stared at her. Then he turned to look after the grogach. He snorted.

"That?" he said. "Who would even speak to a shit-shovelling half-breed? Never mind believe what it said."

"Other half-breeds, humans, fey, minor godlings..." Lenith let her voice trail off. She flipped her hand palm up and shrugged. "In the Palace purity of the Blood might be all that is important, down here it matters less."

"But it still matters," Aphar said.

"Of course," Lenith said. "But not as much, and less when there might be profit at stake. His story will be paid heed too. Still it can't hurt to try and avoid inspiring anymore gossip. Down here."

Lenith took a short cut down an alley. Aphar had to duck to avoid catching his head on the strung washing lines. She stepped out of the alley and into a wide, busy square. It was market day. It was always market day.

Striped canopies fluttered over the weathered shopfronts; the eternal twilight bleached the colours until they were monochrome ghosts. Trestle tables lined every storefront, lined with goods to

T.A. Moore

coax passers-by into purchases

Outside a butcher's shop a Fachan stood, single eye watering from the smoke, tossing shreds of meat, fresh sliced from the carcass and still with the hide on, into a smouldering brazier. When anyone paused near the stall the Fachan would waft the smoke towards them with a big callused hand.

Aphar paused by the stall, , and breathed in the smoke with savour.

"Does the Master want some goods?" the Fachan asked, edging forward and bobbing its head subserviently. "We have the best goods here. Cow and hind, duck and falcon, human rump and demon blood. Anything you want we can get for you, Master."

Lenith stepped in front of Aphar.

"He doesn't want anything," she told the fey creature firmly. "Go back to your trade."

The Fachan butcher wrinkled his lips back from small yellow teeth.

The Even

"But selling is my trade," it said. "The Master was happy enough to sample our wares, surely he can grace our small shop with his presence."

The grovelling bow nearly topped the misbalanced creature over and then it started trying to hop around her.

"The creature is right," Aphar said. "To savour the essence of flesh again after I thought I lost it forever is sweet."

His expectation had an almost physical weight. The assumption that Lenith would cater his whim for him went unsaid only because he didn't think he needed to say it. Lenith cocked her head to the side.

"We have some infant selkie steaks fresh in," The Fachan coaxed. "The flavour can be human or seal, depending in whether you skin it or not."

Lenith reached into her pocket and pulled out a handful of staters. One of them glinted tarnished silver. She held it up for the Fachan to see. He ran his wide, wet tongue over his lips and blinked eagerly, his lid stretching over the damp bulge of his eyeball.

"Oh yes, Mistress," he said. "I will fetch you a cut of our finest meat: sliced near the bone, sweetly marbled and still wearing its infant skin."

He reached for the coin. Lenith snapped it back, tucking it against her palm.

"For this," she said. "I could buy every shank and brisket that you have sliced in that shop. Do you know Oelliet's Tallyman, a human and new, relatively so."

"I know him," the Fachan said.

"Then give me a slab of dog," Lenith said. "And get a message to the Tallyman, Faceless Lenith wants to see him, where we met before."

The Fachan rolled his eye around uncertainly. Lenith waited. Finally he nodded and held his hand out. The palm was deeply lined and his fingers, slightly curled, were crusted with dirt and old blood. Lenith dropped the coin into his hand. He tucked it into his apron and got a slab of meat from under the stall. The back of the slice was covered with thick skin and ginger hair. The Fachan wrapped it up in waxed paper and tied it with string. He was surprisingly deft with his single hand.

"I know where the Tallyman resides," he said. "But I cannot leave until the other assistant gets here. It will be a quarter-hour, perhaps a short while more. As soon as he gets here, I'll take your message."

He held the package out. Lenith took it and handed it to Aphar. He stared at it, his nostrils flared, like he'd never carried anything before. Maybe he hadn't. For a moment he looked like he was going to throw it down. He thought better of it. Perhaps his new situation had sunk in after all.

Lenith left the Fachan to his work and walked briskly down the street, trailed by a sullen Aphar. She passed a couple of shops till she found one that sold bolts of cloth and old clothes. The shopkeeper sucked her teeth when Lenith gave her a handful of coins. She would have bargained but Lenith wasn't in the mood.

"A cloak," Lenith said. "One big enough to cover him. Other than that I don't care."

"For a few coppers more..." the shopkeeper started to say.

"Get me the cloak or give me the money back," Lenith said impatiently.

The shopkeeper sucked her teeth some more and went into the back of the shop. She came back with an untreated, grey wool cloak that, when Lenith shook it out, was long enough to cover Aphar from skull to the ground. He put it on and drew the hood up. It reached to his nose. Only his chin and his broad, white hands were visible.

Lenith reached up and tugged the hood down even further.

"It'll do," she said.

"Grey," Aphar lifted the edge of the cloak and looked at the loose woven, dove-coloured material. "Appropriate to my new condition and station, I suppose."

Lenith led them back onto the street. Her bloody shirt had dried on her skin. It itched.

"It is serviceable," she said. "For now, it will do. Perhaps the

The Even

Tallyman's master will dress you in cloth-of-gold and manacle you with gems."

Aphar snorted and then drew the cloak tighter around his body. His bare feet left smears of blood on the cobbles. He walked slowly, letting Lenith lead, and turned his head from side to side, studying the others in the street.

"You have a better view down here than in a litter," he said.

Lenith slowed down until he caught up with her.

"I had not thought that the lower caste Yekumi left the Palace often," she said.

Aphar wasn't looking at her; his attention was on a satyr bartering furiously over a love potion. He answered absently.

"We do not," he said. "I only came down to indulge my lover. She had friends who would not be welcome in the Palace and she wanted me to meet them. It seemed little enough to do in return for staying in her favour."

Lenith held up a hand to silence him.

"Tell me the rest when we are inside," she said.

Seventeen

Three demons founded the City under the Even Stone.

Twelve-winged Sammael who found the Even stone. He was the most wicked of the Fallen Thrones, tempter of Eve and the Demon of the North Wind, the gall bearing Angel of Death.

When he worked out what the great, carved stone was he rode the winds to the dark, mirrored cave where his wife resided. Lilith, the Maiden of Desolation, listened to his tale and then rose from her mourning couch. She drew a cloak of flames over her shoulders and bound her brilliant garnet hair back with exactly forty ornaments less one.

They flew back to the Even but Yekum, he who had seduced all the

The Even

sons of heaven into tasting the flesh of the Daughters of Eve, saw them pass and followed. All three arrived at the Even at the one time, slipping through the fold in the fabric of the world, and laid claim to what they found there. A nascent city, the petals of stone buildings and highways unfolding like their attention was like sunlight to a rose.

At first they warred over the city, feeding the unfolding streets with hot, black blood. When that settled nothing they tried negotiation and divided the city into sectors.

Sammael's sector hived with the dead and the streets ran red with blood.

Lilith sector's was like a hothouse bloom, lush, sensual and with a lingering odour of corruption.

Yekum's sector grew as it would while the Seducer amused himself with his consorts and his many children.

All of that was millennia-old history: before the plagues of Egypt, before Lot's wife turned to salt and Lot's children turned to their father's bed.

Over time Sammael and Lilith grew bored with the city and absented themselves. Yekum claimed the City for himself. His co-rulers sectors he left to atrophy, overrun by the chaotic growth of the city. Remnants survive: the Courtyards of Death towards the west of the city where wormwood carpets the ground and the hungry Red Throne brothels where only the most desperate and deviant seek surcease.

Since then, the Yekum's iron whim ruled the city. The myriad half-breed clans of his children contest for power under him. The Yekumi scheme and plot, crafting complex labyrinthine schemes of betrayal and double crosses, only to see it all shattered with casual cruelty by their father.

The beings that live in the City are so far below them as to not exist. What influence could a deposed legend, a weary merrow or a guilt-stricken fragment of a goddess have on the schemes of the lofty Yekumi?

Eighteen

Lenith's residence was currently a small temple of smoke-stained sandstone. One of the slender pillars that supported the roof had already been cracked, chunks of stone littering the porch. It changed regularly, as everything in the City changed, but the disrepair always remained the same. Lenith kicked the chunks of stone out of the way and led the way inside.

There were few furnishings in the room: a high-backed, lounging couch, a table, a fire-pit and a locked cabinet. The walls were decorated in bright murals portraying Greek Gods strutting arrogantly across the Styx and in Egypt. That was the City's choice, not Lenith's. She thought it had been chosen to annoy her.

She took her jacket off and tossed it onto the couch. It landed on the arm, hung there for a moment and then dropped to the ground in a tangle of leather. Lenith didn't bother to pick it up.

"Make yourself comfortable," she told Aphar. "If you are still hungry then light the firepit."

Aphar looked around.

"Slaves in the Palace live better than this," he said. "The dead in the Palace have finer quarters than this."

Lenith pulled her t-shirt out of her jeans. She glanced around her home and tried to see it as he did. By Aphar's standards she supposed it was spartan. In fact, by Spartan standards it was spartan. Still, it suited her needs. She didn't concern herself that much with luxury. Not that she had the funds to indulge herself even if she cared for it.

"The dead spend more time in their grave than I do here," she said. "It is better than the gutter."

He grunted, "I am not sure of that."

"Just amuse yourself," Lenith told him. "I won't be long."

She left Aphar kindling the fire pit and went into the

The Even

antechamber to get changed. It was a store-room more than anything else. There was a couch pushed against the far wall, under a mural of Aphrodite and Ares caught in the net. It was piled high with clothes and various bits and pieces that she had collected here and there, for this and that. No-one could have slept on it but Lenith didn't sleep. Some gods did, but she'd never had the knack.

The smell of burning flesh filled the house. Lenith savoured it, even second-hand. Her stomach rumbled.

She stripped quickly, dropping her bloody shirt and dirty jeans to the floor, and donned clothes that were similar, if not identical, to those discarded. There was a bowl of water on the dresser, left from the other day. Lenith picked up the bowl, bent forwards and tipped the water over her head.

Mud and water dripped onto the floor between her feet. Lenith wiped her hand over her face and squeezed most of the water from her hair. Then she shook her head like a dog, spraying water over the walls and tossed her hair back. The wet ropes of hair were cold against the back of her neck.

A cracked mirror hung on the back of the door. Lenith checked her reflection in it. The crack gave Lenith's featureless face an odd, lopsided cant. It looked like her jaw had been badly broken and healed badly. The mess of blood and dirt smeared over her face didn't help dispel the impression. She dipped a cloth into the dregs of water left in the bowl and wiped her face.

So what next?

A smear of dirt clung to her jaw. She wiped it off with her thumb. The most practical thing to do would be contact the Tallyman and arrange the handover. Aphar would be their concern; so would her debt.

It was dangerous to do anything else. Her refusal to be marked, and the fact she still was, what she was, offered her protection from the petty politicking that was common in the city. If the Yekum was involved, however, things changed. The Yekum had been the least powerful and least malicious of the Triad who ruled the Even, if only because he was engrossed in his own debauchery, but he would not be thwarted. He would not be pleased if he discovered that Lenith had undone his sentence of death. And for all her complaints of boredom, she didn't want to die. Not just yet.

But it wouldn't hurt to find out the answers to a few questions few. Then she could turn Aphar over to his new Master. It was not the dire fate he painted it, most people in the city were owned: one way or another.

She kicked her soiled clothes into the corner and went into the other room. Aphar reclined on the couch, his robe stripped off and wadded under his head, and watched the smoke eddy up from the pit. The coals were glowing red, crumbling into white ash as they burnt out, and the steak had burnt black.

Aphar lifted his head from the arm of the couch.

"It was dog," he said.

Lenith waved his complaint aside dismissively. She perched on the arm of the couch, next to Aphar's feet, and braced her hands on her thighs.

"It will stop you from starving," she said. "If it will comfort you then imagine it was carved from a wolf."

Aphar was still poking his stomach absently. He sneered at Lenith.

"It would not comfort me," he said. "In the Palace they burnt the flesh of human and sphinx for the most casual of meals; the commonest morsel. For feasts the cooks would fetch the sharpest flensing knives and venture down to the cellars. Then in cells they would carve fresh fillets from the captive angels held there. The scent of their flesh, roasted over myrrh, was indescribable. In comparison to that wolf is as pedestrian as dog. And your company a great deal less pleasing than that of my lover and kin."

"Perhaps you will find the Tallyman's Master a more discerning host," Lenith said. She shifted and lifted her feet onto the couch, nudging Aphar's legs out of the way. "I have some questions for you, Aphar."

Aphar lifted his head. The couch creaked and groaned as he shifted his stone burdened weight. He narrowed golden eyes at

The Even

Lenith.

"And if I answer?" he asked. "What do I get in return?"

"You could consider it repayment for your rescue," Lenith said.

Aphar lifted his eyebrows. "So you have a sense of humour after all."

It was a fair comment. Lenith nodded in acknowledgement of it. Even if she hadn't been getting paid, no one counted a debt in the City unless it was sealed before-hand. Not unless they were a fool. Apparently Aphar was not, despite his recent misfortunes, that.

"What do you want then?" she asked.

Aphar shifted his attention to the fire. It was burning out, turning grey around the edges. Occasionally a dribble of fat or charred skin dropped from the burning meat, making the coals flare. The dancing sparks reflected in Aphar's eyes. He breathed in slowly, seeking steadiness or just the last threads of smoke from the meat.

"I'll tell you my story," he said. "If you don't surrender me to the Tallyman."

Lenith rubbed her chin and thought about it.

"I won't promise that," she said. "Your story might hold no interest to me. Why should I risk angering two powerful beings in our society in return for a banal account of a Yekumi's fall from favour? The Yekum finds fault with his children all the time. They rarely fall so far as you, but they fall."

Aphar stared at her. Then he gave a humourless bark of laughter.

"That is your greatest fear?" he said. "That my story might bore you? Not the debt that's on your head or the punishment for welchers?"

Lenith lent forwards, bending over her legs, and rested her folded arms on her knees.

"The Tallyman has a wealthy Master," she said. "But her minions are of low quality. He was new-come to the city, or relatively so, and was... clumsy."

There was silence as Aphar worked that through in his head. When he did realize what she meant he didn't believe it.

"He slit the throat before the bowl was ready?" he asked.

Lenith nodded.

"I swore to fetch you back," she admitted. "After that, anything I do for them is a courtesy."

A smile twitched at the corner of Aphar's mouth. His relief was palpable, if premature.

"And are you known for your courtesy?" he asked lightly.

"Yes," Lenith said quietly. The lightness drained from Aphar's face. "But give me reason to be discourteous and I will consider it."

Aphar's mouth tightened to a thin line. He turned his gaze away from her and shook his head.

"Not good enough," he said. "Why should I amuse you for the promise of a maybe? I am no jester to caper for coins."

Lenith laced her fingers together and tapped her thumbs. She waited. So did Aphar. When he didn't speak after a couple of minutes Lenith sat back. Her poker face was, by necessity, excellent; if Aphar had not conceded so far then he wouldn't.

"I cannot promise not to give you to the Tallyman's Master," she said. He stiffened and glared at her with feral golden eyes. Lenith didn't let him speak. "Enough, Nameless. Don't be a fool and make me swear to something that's not in your interest. The Tallyman's Master might be the best of your choices. But I won't hand you over to your enemies."

Aphar grabbed the back of the couch and pulled himself up. The stubs on his shoulders moved, trying to steady himself with wings that were no longer there.

"You are the one who said that I had no friends left in the City," he said. "Who else would be but an enemy?"

"Neutrality is not the same as enmity," Lenith said. "You've reached the limits of my curiosity. Do you accept or not?"

He didn't answer immediately. His hand flexed around the back of the couch, making the wood creak. At last, he nodded.

"I'll tell you my story then," he said. "For what it's worth. All I

The Even

know is what happened, not the truth behind it."

Lenith gestured for him to go on.

Instead of doing so immediately Aphar rested his cheek against his knuckles. He looked distant, his attention was somewhere else.

"I was there, I saw it all, but even now it makes no sense," he said. "There must have been strands connecting events behind the scene but I was neither high-ranked nor wise enough to see them. Despite what you believe of the Palace, Lenith, not everyone cares to play politics. I was low-clan, son of a daughter of a daughter of the Yekum. No-one cared to court my influence since I had none."

"You were the Yekum's cup-bearer," Lenith said. That much the Heralds from the Palace had shared. "That is a prestigious position."

Aphar shrugged one broad shoulder. He scratched at a rivulet of stone that ran down over his chest.

"No virtue of mine won me the post," he said. "It was a courtesy to my lover. She was high in the Yekum's favour. At least, then..."

He trailed off and shrugged. It wasn't really necessary to explain further. The Yekum, jaded and debauched and ancient, had neither loyalty nor staying power to his favourites. Lovers, kin or both passed in and out of his regard like Kore through the Deathlands.

"What was the plot?" Lenith asked. "The heralds were so sparing in their details about it that most people assumed the Yekum was simply executing you on a whim."

Aphar shifted. He sighed and rubbed at the back of his neck.

"I am so weighty, now," he said. "It is wearying. As for the Heralds, I am unsurprised that they were circumspect. There was no benefit to the Palace in letting it be known that a plot to dethrone the Yekum had so nearly succeeded."

Lenith cocked her head sharply to the side, her dreads rustling. There were always plots in the Palace but most were internecine struggles between the clans of the Yekum's children. Plots against the Yekum lasted only as long as they amused him. For his ennui and debauchery he was still one of the Fallen, he had learnt treachery from the mouth of the first Treacher himself.

"How nearly?" she asked.

Aphar was still rubbing the back of his neck. He smiled thinly.

"Too nearly for it to ever work again," he said. "A poison brewed by Gula, the Mistress of Poisons herself, although she denied knowing what it would be used for. It was a vile brew. It might not have killed the Yekum but it would have weakened him surely."

"Enough to topple him from the Throne?"

Aphar held his hand out and wobbled it slightly from side to side. "Perhaps or perhaps not. It is what the plotters hoped surely."

"But the Yekum did not drink?"

"No. He let his consort sip from the cup ahead of him. She was a simple thing, no god or demon. The poison scoured her from the inside. She died, and badly. Because I was the cup-bearer, because I had put the cup in the Yekum's hand, they blamed me for it. Then, when they searched my room, they found a vial with traces of the poison secreted amongst my belongings. But I swear I knew nothing of the crime. I was content with my lot. Someone framed me for the crime."

He fell into a brooding silence.

"Who?"

Aphar shrugged

"Everyone has their own scheme brewing," Aphar said. "Perhaps some clan mother actually planned to kill the Yekum and take his place. Perhaps one of his enemies seduced or bought a servant of the Palace to pour the poison. Or perhaps the crime was never meant to succeed and it was just designed to drive me and my lover even further from the Yekum's favour. Not that Tanit needed any help in antagonising the Yekum."

Lenith leant forwards slightly.

"Tanit of Sarepta?" she said. "Your lover has fallen sharply from the Yekum's esteem of late. Was the poisoning the cause of that?"

The Even

Aphar full mouth twisted sourly. He shook his head.

"No, Tanit herself was behind that," he said. "She changed in the past two quarters: made new allies, became sentimental and defied the Yekum. At first, he was amused but then his patience left him. Her sentimentality got the best of her during an audience. Some Intulo was condemned for selling ailing beasts for sacrifice and as punishment he was bound to Sopono, the marks cut onto his face. Tanit argued to free him, on the grounds of friendship, and when she was refused she lost her wits. She called the Yekum a ten-horned beast and that his reign would crumble like clay. After that, Tanit was shunned by all."

"So, you don't think that she could be the one who sent for you?"

Aphar shook his head.

"No," he said. "Even if she cared to save me, she would not have the means any longer."

Lenith nodded thoughtfully. She sat for a while, turning the information over in her head. Then she swung her legs around and stood up.

"You should rest," she said, tugging her shirt straight. "Regain your strength."

Aphar grunted and waved a hand at the still smouldering fire pit. "With only dog remains to savour? Where are you going?"

"I have some business affairs to attend to."

"Selling me?"

"I have not decided yet," Lenith said. "I'll fetch you back something more flavourful than dog."

Aphar sat up and leant forwards, the folds of his kilt draping his thighs.

"You're going to just leave me here?"

Lenith picked up her jacket and pulled it out. The leather smelt of grave dirt and blood. It fit the lean lines of her body like a glove, moulded to her shape after years of wear.

"Why not?" she said. "It's not like you have anywhere else to go. Or I have anything it would be worth your while stealing."

She left him sitting there, his elegant features set in a scowl,

T.A. Moore

and let the door slam behind her. It was quiet on the street. A rat, foraging amidst the leavings at the side of the road, rolled a wild, black eye at her. It spun around, a finger clutched in its teeth, and scurried away. At some point in the past its tail had been bitten off. It just had a stump there now.

Lenith stepped down off the steps and turned to the right. She stopped.

The Tallyman stood in the middle of the street. His hands hung loose at his sides. Oelliet's blue mark had been scrubbed off. The black marks beneath looked dark against his red skin. His lips skinned back from his teeth in a smile.

He had nothing to smile about.

Lenith swore and started to turn. It hit her before she could see who was behind it; a tidal wave of inimical power backed up with a cosh to the back of the skull. She landed hard, her face bouncing off the cobbles, and everything went black.

Nineteen

The wind woke her up.

Someone had whistled up a wind and lost mastery of it. Now it was building itself into a gale, howling around the narrow streets and tossing garbage over Lenith's prone body.

She groaned and reached around to feel the back of her head. There was a depression instead of a lump. That was never good. Lenith traced the imprint of whatever had hit her with her fingertips. It hurt, hot and white in her skull, when she pressed on it, but it was healing. She could feel the bone move under her fingers.

The wind caught her jacket and tossed it over her head. Cold, airy gusts made the back of her t-shirt bell. Lenith groaned and rolled over. She pushed her jacket away from her head and sat up.

In a fairytale it would have been a field of wildflowers that surrounded her. This was Even, though, and the city disliked anachronisms that were not its doing. So there were weeds cracking the cobbles and letting their pallid roots run wild; mould and fungus that sprouted in thick carpets on every available surface.

Including Lenith.

She scrambled up off the ground and scraped most of the feathery white mould off her jeans and jacket. Tendrils of it hung from the ends of her hair too, turning her dreadlocks into Spanish moss. She stripped it off on her back into the house

Her couch was shattered and the coals from the fire pit were scattered over the floor. If the temple had been wood this time the whole place would have burnt down. Instead there was charcoal everywhere and charred circles on the floor.

Aphar was gone.

That was hardly unexpected.

Lenith walked over to the remains of the couch. She turned the debris over with the toe of her boot. There were a few shed feathers, shattered where the stone pinions hit the ground, and the ground remnants of the charred dog. And one other thing.

A single, dark red rose petal lay under the cracked arm of the couch, trodden into the ground. Lenith crouched down and peeled it up from the stone. It had torn under someone's heel but it was still nearly the size of her palm, and it was red as blood.

Lenith flicked it away from her and stood up. She rubbed her hands clean on her hips and looked around. Her temper boiled dark and stormy, a pressure against her ribs. Did the Tallyman and his Master imagine this was over? That fear of the Yekum finding out her involvement would lead her to just accept being swindled?

She was Lenith, the Faceless Lily of the Deathlands, and she would not be played for a fool by beings that had been nothing but the demons of some semetic, deep desert tribe in her day. No-one cheated Death and won.

They'd learn that.

Lenith gave the shattered couch a kick, turned on her heel and stalked out into the vegetation-laden street. The wind, picking up an icy edge from her anger, tore at the spindly, force-grown plants.

It pushed Lenith backwards, tugging savagely at her hair and tangling weeds around her legs. She had to duck her head and turn her shoulders into it to make any headway.

At the end of Nix Lane the wind changed direction abruptly, as if it was trying catch her off guard. It caught her squarely in the chest and threw her back. She staggered and hit the wall, bruising her shoulders.

A gremlin, squeaking and swearing all the way, blew down the road, ass over huge, spiky ears. She pushed herself off the wall and grabbed it by the scruff of neck. It swung from her hand, kicking and clawing. She lifted it up so it was even with her face.

It sucked in its cheeks, ready to spit at her. She shook it hard enough to make it swallow, choking and coughing on its own

The Even

sputum.

"Don't," she warned it.

It rolled a bile-yellow eye at her and swallowed hard. Then it opened its mouth, lolling its tongue and showing needle-sharp teeth, to show it was empty. She shook it again to make it close its mouth, which it did with a clicking sound.

"I'm looking for a fey," she said.

It managed a shrug, its sharp shoulder bones poking her hand.

"There's lot of fey in the city," he said. Its voice sounded nails on a blackboard. "I see them all over: here and there, thither and thon."

"I want one in particular," Lenith said. "Thistle, the last time I saw him, he was at Enbilulu's Bait."

The gremlin shrugged again.

"One fey looks much the same as another to me," it said, rolling into a ball and picking its nose with its toenail. "How can I be expected to tell one from the other?"

Lenith waited until it finished eating. Then she smacked it off the wall to give it some motivation. It sneezed a bubble of blood from its nose, spattering Lenith's shirt.

"I don't have time for this," she said. The edge to her voice made the gremlin whine. "I am looking for Thistle Cicerbeta, bound to Tanit of Saerepta. Now where is he?"

The gremlin licked blood from its nose.

"The Eidolon Inn," it said. "An Abaasy pack is fighting the Lord of the Massacre. The betting is running hot."

Lenith felt the sharp, fish-hook in the gut, quirk of interest at that. It took an effort of will to remind herself that she had other matters at hand to deal with first.

"Thistle should be there," the gremlin said. It hadn't noticed her distraction. "His hunger for the wager has surpassed even yours, Faceless. Are we done?"

"We're done."

Lenith loosened her fingers and tossed the gremlin away from her, releasing it into the roaring wind. The gremlin flapped its wings frantically but the wind caught it, tossed it and slammed it into the wall. Its wings crumpled, folding over, and it slid to the ground. Curses spewed from its mouth, damning Lenith's parentage.

She ignored it and turned around to head for the Eidolon. When she reached Bellwether Street there was a bare plot where the inn used to be. A gaggle of children were playing football in the empty lot. The chipped skull they used for a ball skidded over the hard, packed down earth, chased intently by the pack of children. One of them noticed Lenith and peeled away from the crowd.

"Looking for the Eid?" he asked, squinting up at her. Strands of dirty, lank black hair straggled over his bony, tusked face. She nodded. He grinned, showing off gappy white teeth. "Gimme a stater and I'll tell you where it went."

"Or I could find it myself," Lenith said.

"Take you longer," the boy said.

The back of Lenith's head felt hot and heavy with blood still and the magic of the Tallyman's Master made her skin itch. She wasn't in the mood to haggle, and she didn't have time for it either.

"Here." She tossed him a battered sliver of a coin. He snatched it out of the air and wrinkled his nose when he realized how little it was. Lenith pointed a finger at him. "Do not think to test me. It's

The Even

the wrong time for it. Where's the Eidolon?"

The boy sniffed the stater to check for traces of magic. When all he smelt was metal he tucked it into his pocket.

"Last I heard it was off Widdershins Lane. But that was yesterday; might be there now, might not." He shrugged sloped shoulders. "Ain't heard any complaints about the directions yet."

He turned and threw himself back into the game, tackling the boy who had the skull. They hit the ground, rolling and punching, and the others joined in the scrum. Lenith left before anyone claimed the skull.

It didn't take long to get from Bellwether to Widdershins. If you knew the backstreets, and Lenith did, it was only a few blocks across the city.

The Eidolon was a large, square building with smoke-stained brick walls. In Bellwether it matched the rest of the street. Here it squatted between two towers of polished, seamless metal. Reflections that lured and confused the eye rippled up and around the curved sides of the towers. There were no visible ways in or out of the buildings. Silver wires stitched the two towers together. At random intervals the wires trembled and hummed, like something hidden in the towers had plucked them. Although who, or what, and whether the wires were web or harp wasn't clear.

Lenith pushed the doors open and stepped inside. She paused on the doorstep and looked around. The inn was crowded, full of people jostling to lay their service, wage or soul on the outcome of the fight, and it stunk of old grain, blood and the distinctive musky aroma of a big cat.

It wasn't why she was here but addiction drew Lenith's attention to the cage hung in the middle of the room.

Four crossed chains, each thick as a man's wrist and dark with rust, attached it to the rafters. In the corner closest to her the Lord of the Massacre crouched at bay. His tail dangled through the bar, the tufted end twitching angrily. He was well-bloodied, with streaks of gore painted down his flanks and gelling his adolescent mane into punk spikes. Despite that he didn't seem seriously

T.A. Moore

injured.

There were three Abaasy left in the cage with him, the bodies of the others hung from the floor of the cage. One of the Abaasy spat at the Lord of the Massacre. The Egyptian god peeled black lips back from sharp teeth and roared. The Abaasy flinched and the Lord of the Massacre laughed.

The outcome of the fight looked decided. None of the tallymen scattered through the crowd would be taking bets on Sekhmet's son to win.

Lenith's fingers still dropped to her pocket, turning over the few stater that were left thoughtfully. The Abaasy might have something in reserve. After all, they must have had reason to think they could win when they challenged the lion-headed god.

The three Abaasy attacked as one, snarling and snapping at the god's flanks. Hooked, steel teeth sliced through his tough hide and their jaws locked. They dangled from his shoulders and thighs, worrying at their mouthful of flesh. The Lord of the Massacre snarled and threw himself against the bars, crushing one of the Abaasy.

Now there were only two creatures and one of them was limping. The odds were too long, even for Lenith. She shook her head in irritation. This was no time to be distracted; there were things she needed to do.

The Even

When Thistle gambled his debts belonged to Choy San Poh. She was a kinder usurer than Oelliet but she would cut people off rather than let their debts grow too vast. That was why Lenith didn't bet with her.

Lenith grabbed a passing barman and tugged him over so she could yell in his ear over the noise of the bar.

"Is Choy's man here?" she asked.

The man's mouth was sewed shut, magic charms hanging from the stitches. He jerked his head instead of speaking, indicating the far left corner of the bar. Lenith kept her hold on his shoulder. She searched the dimly lit back of the bar until she saw Choy's skinny, fox-tailed Tallyman. His clothes were a little shabby and there weren't many people clustered around his stall. Choy was too fair for her own profit.

Lenith let the barman go back about his duties and pushed her way through the crowd. Halfway across the bar she thought better of the direct approach. Thistle wouldn't want to see her. She ducked around the bulk of a centaur, ignoring the irritated whisk of his tail against her arm, and made her way along the wall.

"Sorry," the Kitsune said, showing white teeth in a wide smile. He gathered up the short stacks of coin on his tray. "Betting's closed."

Thistle's lips pulled back from its teeth in a grimace. It spat a curseword at the Kitsune and turned to go. Lenith put her arm out to stop it.

"Thistle," she said. "We need to have words, you and I."

It gave her a panicked look out of oak-leaf green eyes and ran. Lenith swore, caught flat-footed, and then gave chase. The crowd should have given the skinny, hunch-postured fey the advantage, it was made for squirming through tight spaces. But the crowd opened up before Lenith. No-one sane wanted to cross Death over something as unimportant as giving way in a pub.

Thistle leapt onto the swinging cage. It clung to the bars with hands and feet both. Lenith grabbed for it but she couldn't quite reach its skinny ankle. She cursed viciously, and with enough venom that the worst injured of the Abaasy faltered and died, and Thistle skittered higher.

It almost reached safety. Then a big, black-clawed hand grabbed it by the neck and tossed it back down to the ground. It landed hard, over-jointed limbs sprawling, and Lenith put her foot on its chest before it could recover. The Lord of the Massacre stared down at both of them with mad, amber eyes.

"My thanks," Lenith said politely.

He snarled and shook his head, making his mane bristle. "Stay out of my fights," he growled in a rough, forced voice. "I need no help."

Lenith bowed slightly. "I never thought you did."

He grunted and dropped back to all fours, turning his attention back to his last opponent. Lenith looked down at Thistle. He grimaced up at her and grabbed her ankle. His thin, nailless fingers squeezed the leather of her boots, pinching the flesh and bone beneath.

"Faceless," it said. "I had not expected to see you again. I heard you were gone like the geese in winter."

Lenith leant her weight on its chest and felt its bones creak. It writhed and gasped, bare feet drumming the floor. The other patrons ostentatiously didn't notice them, although Lenith had no doubt rumours would soon fly.

"And is that why you ran?"

Thistle let go her ankle and shrugged, spreading its hands placatingly.

"We argued, last we spoke," it said. "I feared you might hold a grudge."

Lenith crouched down over him, resting her arms on her knee. He chewed on his thin lips and darted his eyes nervously from

The Even

side to side.

"I do," she said. "But I don't think it's against you, Thistle. It's your Master's name that I keep stumbling over, Thistle. Tanit of Saerepta. Her touch has been all over the events of the last few days, like a rash."

Thistle made a sudden, desperate attempt to get away, bucking and squirming like a gaffed fish. Lenith shifted her weight, replacing her foot with her knee, and grabbed a handful of its rough, bristly hair. She slammed its head into the ground a few times until it stopped struggling.

"Listen to me and listen well, Thistle," Lenith said. "Your Master chose to make an enemy of me. It's up to you whether I'm yours too."

Thistle groaned weakly. His head lolled to the side, blood and spit drooling from his slack mouth. Lenith slapped him lightly across the face.

"Stop playacting," she said. "You're no mummer and I know your kind are hardier than that."

Thistle opened his eyes and glared up at her. He licked the blood from his mouth and swallowed.

"And you should know that I can't tell you anything about my Master," he said. "She owns me. I'm loyal."

Lenith grabbed its scant chin between finger and thumb and turned its face so it was looking at her.

"This is Even City," she said. "Brats pimp their mothers on the streets and in the Palace there's not a back without a knife in it. There is no loyalty here. Only debts and contracts. You already tried to warn me off, however poorly done it was. So now we're going to talk, and you'll find a way to tell me what I want to know. Or I'll send you down to the Deathlands with such a geas on you that you'll wish you never ran from the tithe. Understood?"

Thistle spat at her but there was no real defiance left in him. She ignored the gob of phlegm on her shirt and waited. Thistle went limp under her knee and nodded slightly.

"Understood," it sighed.

T.A. Moore

Lenith stood up, pulling it with her. She scruffed the back of its neck like a struggling cat and dragged it over to the door. In the cage the Lord of the Massacre pinned the Abaasy under one, big hand and watched it struggle. Then he lifted his fingers and let it run again: playing.

The wind had reached Widdershins. It plucked an eerie tune on the vibrating strings of the web, or harp. The two towers trembled and hummed like tuning forks. Lenith dragged Thistle down the street till she found an alley. She pushed it in and up against the wall.

"Tanit's hand has been behind everything in this. She made her lover cupbearer and he tried to poison the Yekum. The Tallyman who hired me to retrieve the lover was hers too, under Oelliet's paint. I saw her mark on him when she attacked me in my home and stole Aphar away." She grabbed Thistle's arm with her free hand and held it up, showing it the mark. "This mark. So what is it, Thistle? What is your Master after?"

Thistle giggled, a high-pitched mocking sound.

"My Master?" it said. "Your hands might be bare, Faceless, but you danced to her pipes happily enough. Good dog, heel, sit. All for a coin. The proud Lenith can be bought after all."

Lenith twisted its arm.

"That's not what I asked you," she said.

Thistle writhed and shoved its face into her blank one. It bared needle-teeth and panted, spraying her face with warm, wet spit. The stink of its breath surrounded her.

"There's no point in telling, you know," it said. "It's too late. All will be rue and wormwood and bile and it's all your fault, Faceless. Yours and no-one else's."

"What will be my fault?"

Thistle clicked its mouth shut and sucked his teeth. It slapped at Lenith's hand until she let him go. Then it dropped into its accustomed hunch and straightened its rags, re-layering them to its satisfaction.

"The Yekumi boy," it said. "Tanit's bedmate. Lilim cursed. You fetched him home, tucked him in safe amongst the living? You

The Even

fulfilled the contract?"

Lenith shifted so she stood in front of the entrance to the alley. She crossed her arms and nodded, shrugging at the same time.

"I brought him back," she said. "Your Master broke the contract though. The Tallyman doesn't work for Oelliet and my debt is still outstanding."

Thistle danced forwards and poked its finger hard into Lenith's chest, right on the spot the sword had pierced her.

"Showing your stupidity, Faceless," it said, twisting its finger. "Tanit has kept her word, no one can fault her on that. Debts are of no matter now. You're dead, I'm dead, the boggan that scrapes the shit from the Yekum's chamberpot is dead. Oelliet is dead. It's just that no-one has told us to crawl down in the dirt, not yet."

Twenty

"We will all be dead one day," Lenith said. "It doesn't mean that we can ignore our debts. The City doesn't work that way."

Thistle giggled wheezily and jabbed its finger harder at her chest. This time Lenith pushed it away from her. It hissed and skulked away from her. Lenith turned casually, keeping it well within her field of vision.

"We'll be dead sooner than later," Thistle said. Its eyes were huge and fevered in its brown, bony face. They glittered with malice. It pointed at her. "Thanks to you."

Lenith spread her hands out at her waist and half-bowed. Thistle tried to take advantage of the moment to scuttle past her, but Lenith moved smoothly in front of it. It backed off, head hunched sullenly between its shoulders.

"You grant me too much credit, Thistle," she said. "It has been centuries since I had such an effect on the ebb and flow of life. These days, my influence does not extend beyond one to one connections. Don't make me prove that."

Thistle's back hit the wall. It sank down into a crouch, all sharp and bony angles, and smiled up at her.

"Empty threats, Faceless. We're all dead now. You'd just put me in the ground a little sooner is all." It sniffed the air. "Not much sooner though."

Lenith stared down at him. She'd thought the worst possible outcome would be the Yekum discovering she had aided a traitor escape his punishment. It would have been bad enough. Thistle's terror suggested that there were worse possibilities.

It had been a long time since Lenith felt anything keenly. Even the tug of her gambling addiction dulled after the first hundred years. Some things she'd never felt much in the first place. What did a goddess of death have to fear, for example?

The Even

The sudden cold weight in her gut, replacing the sour twist of spite, that was concern, at least.

"What has Tanit done?" she asked.

Thistle just shook its head violently. "I cannot speak of that. She was most pointed about that, Faceless, most precise. My Master knows that I do not, cannot, share her... conviction."

If she'd thought it would have worked Lenith would have beaten the answer out of him. Unfortunately, that wasn't much of an incentive when Thistle was already convinced death was only a few hours away. Lenith crossed her arms, squeezing her elbows, and considered. After a moment's thought she dropped into a crouch, face to face with Thistle. It sneered and turned its head into its shoulder, away from her.

"If you are playing me, Thistle," she said softly. "I will make you pay for it in full."

Thistle hid his face behind his long, spindly fingers.

"No lies, Faceless. But I cannot tell you more." He parted his fingers and glared at her through the gap. "If only you'd cared enough to listen last time we spoke. Without the Yekumi all their plans would have come to naught but ill-wishes and bile."

Lenith nodded absently.

"Them," she said. "So this is more than Tanit and her minions?"

Thistle gnashed his teeth together.

"I cannot speak of it," he said. "Not the plan, not the planners. I am hers and she made her will clear."

"You can't talk of the plan and you can't talk of the plotters," Lenith said. "Tanit has surely covered her treason well."

There was an incongruous pride in Thistle's nod of agreement. He had been one of Tanit's earliest followers in the city. Even now he couldn't quite shake his loyalty to her, his pride in their reflected accomplishments. Lenith ignored it.

"But I know who, partially, and I can find out why," she said. "So when, Thistle. When do the treachers start to peddle their trade? Did Tanit bind your tongue on that too?"

Thistle dropped his hands slightly, revealing his face from

brow to nose. He peered at her over his fingertips, blinking uncertainly.

"No," he said slowly. "She did not. It is now, this moment. They are setting their plot into motion as we speak. But I cannot tell you why or where."

Lenith stood up smoothly. Her jacket bound under her arms. She tugged her arms loose and raised her face to the sky. The wind spun and flailed above the alley. It had stirred the dull sky into whorls and tossed up every stink and odour from the dregs of the city. Under it all Lenith could smell death. And it wasn't the pretty, perfumed death of the Temples. It was bloody and raw and vast.

"The why I can work out. As for the where..." She rubbed her fingers together, feeling the thick, velvety texture of the petal again. "The where I can work out on my own."

Thistle dropped its head, resting its forehead on its fingertips. "There's no point," it said. "It's too late."

Lenith kicked it, knocking it onto its side in the mud.

"Stop mewling over the ruins of your life," she said. "Nothing is decided until it is in the past."

Thistle rolled to its feet and scrambled by her, hunched and scuttling like a spider. It paused in the mouth of the alley to hiss a prediction of failure at her. Then it was gone. There was the chance that it had gone to warn Tanit but it wasn't likely. Thistle might have stayed within the constraints of its contract, but it had still betrayed Tanit. She would not take that kindly.

That meant that Lenith still had time. Although to do what, she was not yet certain.

For once the City seemed to favour Lenith. The wind was at her back and the Red Throne District was, more or less, where it was meant to be. No road-blocks or lost highways delayed her; the path seemed almost to open for her.

She found she feared the meaning behind that.

It had been a long time, even judged by the City's unreliable timekeeping, since Lilith wearied of the entertainment within the city. Centuries at least. There was still no mistaking the moment

The Even

when Lenith set foot into the District. Reflections of her pale, blank face were cast back from nearly every surface; Lilith had placed her beloved mirrors everywhere that they would fit. There were narrow black houses with no windows or doors and the smell of joyless sex hung in the air. Despite the thick walls sometimes the screams were still loud enough to hear.

Lenith walked quickly through empty streets. There were people in the District, the screams that could occasionally be heard through the thick walls proved that, but even in Even City there were things to be ashamed off. A visit to the Red Throne Brothels was one of them.

There was a garden at the centre of the District. Lilith had dwelt there once. Whatever Tanit was doing, she'd do it there.

Lenith smelt the garden before she saw it, the thick, heady aroma of roses. They'd grown wild. Runners had escaped the confines of the rusted iron fences, spreading down the street and up over the nearby houses. Some of the great, nodding blooms were bigger than her head and the thorns were the length of her hand. They rattled and swayed in the wind, scratching the plaster walls and shedding petals. Fresh roses budded, swelled and flowered to take their place.

Thick red petals carpeted the cobbled street. They tore under Lenith's boots and released a heady, sweetly corrupted smell. It was the same smell that had hung in her house.

She slowed as she approached the great, rusted iron railings. The delicate rods, some no thicker than a child's finger, were twisted into complex, eye-baffling designs. It was tempting to try and pick out the images: a screaming face there, a half-finished rune nearly hidden in the weeds and wild roses. But when Lenith took her attention from an image, however clearly she could see it, and looked back, it was gone. She shook her head and crept up to the fence.

Her fingertips touched the gate and gave it a gentle push. It swung open with a rough, grating sound that made her cringe and freeze. No-one raised the alarm and she relaxed slightly. She slid through the gate, her spare form fitting the gap neatly.

T.A. Moore

A man's clear, passionate voice rose and fell in the rhythms of oration. The heavy growth of roses, thick as a rain forest, stole the fire from his voice, flattening it.

"Behold a great image. A image whose brightness was excellent, and yet whose form was terrible: a head of gold, breast of silver, manhood of brass, legs of iron and feet of clay. Does this not describe the Fallen, Yekum, who rules us so cruelly? Golden-haired, white skinned, common of sex and cursed so that setting foot to the earth will be in his downfall."

There was a low mumble in answer. Whoever spoke sounded less sure of themself than the first speaker. Lenith picked her way down the path, careful of where she put her feet. The crushed rose petals made the footing precarious, although it deadened her footsteps.

The first voice continued: "This world and all in it are but chaff, waiting to be threshed. The dross, the iron and brass and dirt, will be discarded. The pure will be lifted on the wind and taken to His bosom. So it has been promised. Think of it and make your choice. What would you rather do, dwell in eternal paradise or wallow here in filth and dissipation? The sins of the Father shall be passed to the son, child. You carry the sins of the Yekum on your shoulders, each pebble a betrayal and each vein a crime."

Lenith was closer this time, close enough to recognise the voice. Aphar

"He is the Yekum: my progenitor."

This time a woman spoke.

"Is he?" There was an arch lilt to her voice. "You have been cast off and denied, my love. Thrown to the wolves in the most literal of ways. All that awaits you now is a lifetime as a pariah, the lowest of the low. Those who once danced to your whim and delighted in the smallest sign of your favour will look down on you."

Lenith reached the edge of the clearing and stopped, still in the shadows. There were ten or fifteen beings, many of them clinging to the shadows just as she did, gathered in the small, paved courtyard. About half of them were human, strange enough on its

The Even

own since Lilith never had any love for the children of husband's second wife. The others were a cross-section of the lesser races in the City: goblins and sluagh and horned tarbh uisge. The three speakers stood in front of the fountain. Two of them, Aphar and Tanit, Lenith had expected to see. The third surprised her.

"Prester John."

Tanit turned, the silken folds of her gown floating, and raised her hand. Jewelled bangles slid down her arm and gold and gems glittered on her fingers. Prester John caught her wrist, his fingers dark against her skin.

"No," he said.

A pout turned the corners of Tanit's lush, crimson mouth down at the corners. Her narrow, kohl-painted eyes narrowed spitefully. She flexed her fingers.

"She's dangerous."

Prester John smiled tiredly. He lowered Tanit's hand back to her side gently.

"So are we all," he said with a sigh. "So are we all, Tanit. There is no need for more violence. This will all be over soon enough."

Emotions flickered over Tanit's hard, lovely face. Finally, she licked her lips with a pale, pointed tongue and nodded. She bent her head, dark hair falling over her face.

"As you say, Prester. No more violence." He patted her shoulder approvingly. Tanit cast a sidelong, spiteful look at Lenith and went over to Aphar. She stroked his arm and murmured to him, her upturned face heavy with sensuality and adoration. Aphar tilted his head to listen, his hair making pale streaks against her dark locks. The other watchers shifted and murmured uncertainly in the shadows.

"Lenith the Etruscan, is it not," Prester John said, drawing Lenith's attention to him.

"Lenith of Etrusca," she corrected him. She sauntered over to the fountain and sat down. One hand trailed in the water, tracing patterns in the rose-tainted algae. "I was no mortal, to let a land lay claim to me, I claimed it.."

A flick of John's hands dismissed the importance of the

correction. He stepped forward to stand in front of her. His robes were still ragged and feet bare but he looked triumphant despite that, as if he had already won.

"Lenith, either way," he said. "This isn't your place, Lenith. There is nothing for you here."

"What are you doing, Prester?" Lenith asked. "Why are you a part of this?"

He opened his mouth, holding his hands out. Then he paused, dropped his hands to his sides and shrugged slightly.

"I could lie, but why bother now. I'm not a part of this, Lenith. I am this. We all are. This is what the Fifth Men have sought for centuries." He leant down and caught Lenith's hands. "Freedom. For everyone. At last, we'll all be free."

The word rippled through the clearing, repeated by the other beings with various degrees of hope and fear. Even Tanit, her face bright with belief, mouthed the word. Of them all, she should know better. She had been a god, gods did not believe in things. It was not their function.

Lenith let her hands rest limply in Prester John's.

The Even

"Free," she said. "That's not what Thistle said. He said it was death you were working on here. Death for everyone in the City."

Prester John let go of her hands. He turned and stared over the city, at the glistening spires and the muddily tiled roofs of the District. His wide mouth twisted with disgust.

"And is not about time? It is a sewer civilisation we have nurtured here, Lenith. Ruled by a demon, devouring ourselves, sunk in a glut of debauchery and vice. And this is for eternity, since time does not lower itself to visit here. An eternity of wearying, empty sinning?"

Lenith drew her knee up to her chest, her heel braced on the green-stained marble rim of the fountain.

"You chose to come here."

Prester John turned to glare at her. His face was twisted with old grief and bitterness.

"What other choice did I have?" he asked. "Time does not shy from passing in the true world. Men died, countries changed beyond anything I had dreamed and I, I passed from the memories of men. They denied that I ever existed and painted my kingdom as a fantasy brewed in the minds of the ignorant. There was no place for me anymore. But this city is no fit place to live. I tried to bring salvation to the beings here, I preached the word of God, but they turned their shoulders to me. They would not hear!"

His voice cracked and he stopped. Tanit abandoned Aphar and hurried to sooth Prester John. She stroked his back and cooed to him.

"We listened," she said, resting her face on his shoulder. "All here listened and heard. We believe in your words and in your message."

Prester John reached up and covered her hand with appreciation. They stood there for a moment. Lenith's soft chuckle disturbed them.

"You believe in his madness," she said. Looking over their shoulder she caught Aphar's gaze. "Come away, Aphar. It is bad enough to be labelled a treacher; don't let them make it a reality. You do want to be caught up in this. When the Yekum finds out, he will make the punishment of the curse seem mild."

Out of the corner of her eye Lenith saw Prester John nudge Tanit away, nodding towards Aphar. She caught up her skirts and glided back over to the stone-touched demon. A slim, ringed hand touched his cheek.

"Don't listen to her, my love," she purred. "The Faceless has no love for you, or anyone. She might claim to speak in your best interests but she lied."

Aphar snorted.

"That she never claimed," he said. "But think, Lenith. You laid

The Even

my choices out for me, stark enough. For a crime I didn't commit the Yekum unNamed me. To the City I am nothing, now."

"You were glad enough to return," Lenith said. "When you left the Deathlands you said you would never leave the City again. Now you listen to some insanity about death and freedom from a Christian wether-king? Were you so enamoured of the Deathlands that you want to return?"

Doubt creased Aphar's face. It was Prester John who spoke to him this time.

"Do not heed her, Aphar," he said. "She is a pagan spirit, sent to tempt us from righteousness."

Lenith mocked.

"Unlike Tanit," she said. "She who used to glut herself on the flesh of the first-born children of her worshippers?"

Prester John drew himself up. He glared at Lenith with blistering disgust. She weathered it easily.

"Tanit has heard my words and come to the light," he said. "She has repented for her sins. Once we have ended this world and brought the fifth king to His throne at last, she will abandon her godhood and assume humanity."

Lenith shuddered. The thought made her stomach curdle. From the sudden grimace on Aphar's face he felt the same way.

"Human?" he said.

Prester John turned smoothly, holding his hands out. "Not you," he said. "You are not a pagan, nor have you ever seduced the hearts of men from the worship of their God. After this world ends, and we, who brought the prophecy to completion, sup in paradise, you will be risen to the rank of angel. You will outrank, in God's eyes, all of the Fallen spirits, even the Yekum."

Lenith stood up and stepped forwards. Without looking around Prester John snapped his fingers. The largest of his Fifth Men followers slid from the shadows and moved towards her. She stopped and held up her hands.

"You said no violence, Prester," she reminded him.

He half-turned to look at her. His familiar paternal smile was on his face but his eyes were cold.

"Unless it is necessary," he said. "I have no desire to harm you, Lenith. If you will not heed the truth of my words then you will be gone soon enough. But I will not have you interfere. This is Aphar's decision."

Lenith sat back down. She folded her legs under her and rested her hands on the sharp points of her knees.

"Guided by you," she said.

"Guided by the voice of wisdom," Tanit said.

Lenith went to say something else but changed her mind. She needed to know what Prester John planned. He was known, although not respected, as a moral man about the City. He had a way about him. His Fifth Men, with their preaching and pleas for compassion, were viewed with amusement but there were always those who joined him. Lenith had never heard anything to suggest that he was planning to commit mass-murder by apocalypse. So she wrapped her hands around her knees and listened.

"I...I do not know," Aphar said.

Tanit pressed herself against the hard line of his body. She reached up and pressed her hand against his face, drawing his gaze down to her.

"You have to, my love," she said. "You're our only hope."

Prester John gestured. A wiry knocker stepped from between the thick, thorned stems. A pick-axe hung from the Cornish fey's callused, hand, the brutal spike angled towards the ground. The knocker held it out to Prester John.

"You're the only one who can do this," Prester John said. "For as the prophecy describes the Yekum, it also describes you, Aphar. You shall be the one to break the stone and shatter this kingdom, releasing the flood that will wash us all clean."

Lenith stiffened. She tried to jump to her feet but the watchful Fifth Men grabbed her. They muffled her face with their hands and hobbled her arms and legs.

Prester John knelt in front of Aphar. He held the pickaxe up, balanced across his arms, and bowed his head humbly.

"Lead us to paradise, Aphar," he said. "Without you the prophecy will never be fulfilled. We will languish here forever,

The Even

trapped in this clay flesh."

The other Fifth Men, those not holding Lenith, bowed down too. Soon only Tanit and Aphar stood. She draped herself against his side and stroked his stomach, whispering encouragement.

Aphar reached out and hesitated. He looked to Lenith. She shook her head at him. His eyes flickered in acknowledgement. Then he closed his fingers around the worn, sweat-stained handle of the pickaxe. He lifted it up and tested the weight with a few truncated swings.

"In this new world I will be honoured?" he asked.

"Of course," Prester John promised smoothly. "Over all your kind."

Aphar nodded slowly. "Then I'll do it."

"Then go," Prester John said, looking up. He scrambled to his feet. The knees of his robe were stained with mud and red petals. He flung out his arm, pointing to the Palace. "You are the stone in my hand, Aphar. Smash your father's kingdom; make room for the new throne."

Tanit crowed with delight. She caught Aphar's face and dragged him down for a kiss. The air rippled around them. Between one breath and the next they were gone.

Twenty-One

The Fifth Men holding onto Lenith slackened their grip. She shrugged them off and stalked over to Prester John. He stood with his back to her, gazing at the spot where Tanit had stood. Lenith grabbed his shoulder and pulled him round to face her. There were tears still on his cheeks but he looked content. Satisfied.

"What have you done?" Lenith asked.

Prester John brushed her hand off his shoulder as if it was nothing. He smiled at her.

"Something you cannot undo," he said. "Make your peace, Lenith. You have little enough time to do it. The prophecies will be fulfilled and the world will end."

"We'll be free." The murmur rose from the Fifth Men.

"You'll be dead," Lenith said. "Try it first, before you claim you'll be free."

She turned and started to push her way through the crowd. They made no attempt to get out of her way but parted under the press of her hands. The ecstatic glitter in their eyes and flush to their cheeks were familiar. All of them believed in Prester John's prophecies and promises.

Damn the man.

"Do not waste your time," Prester John called after her. "Tanit will have taken Aphar to where he needs to be. You will never get there in time, even if you work out where it is."

Did he think she was a fool? Lenith turned around and took a step towards Prester John. She pointed at him with a pale hand, the shadows of the roses tattooed on the back of her hand.

"I am neither deaf nor stupid, Prester," she said. "Your plan is transparent. There is only one flood in the City that waits to be released. But I doubt that the Yekum will need my aid in thwarting it. The wards around the Even Stone have been built like a wall over the centuries, one atop the other. No-one but the Yekum can get near."

"I know," Prester John said. "No-one can get near. The wiles of men and demons cannot thwart prophecy, Lenith. Goodbye. We won't meet again."

He bowed slightly, inclining from the waist. Then he walked past Lenith and out of the courtyard. The rest of the Fifth Men disappeared too, fading into the shadows and stealing away. Lenith was left alone in the garden. She rubbed her hand through her hair, the texture coarse against her palm, and repeated her own words again.

"No-one," she said. "No-one, of course."

She took a step towards the gate, back the way she'd come, and stopped. Prester John might be a fool in many ways, but he was right about how long it would take her to get across the city. The District was on the outskirts of the city: always. The Even was in the centre: always.

If the City continued to favour her she could get to Even Square in half a mark. Maybe less. It still wouldn't be swiftly enough.

Lenith sat down on the edge of the fountain. She rested her hands on her knees and bent her head. The roses stirred around her; the great, layered blooms bowing predatorily.

Prester John seemed to have forgotten that Tanit was not the only goddess in the garden that night. Perhaps he thought that Lenith's rarely used powers had faded or he imagined that she had never shared Tanit's level of puissance.

He was wrong.

There was a price to pay, there was always a price to pay, but her powers were still hers to command.

One of the rose stems slid over the tiled, weedy paving stones. It wrapped itself around her ankle and tightened. The long black thorns pierced the leather of her boots and dug into the skin beneath. Blood spilt and started to fill Lenith's boot. Another whip-thin branch caught her arm and yet another wrapped around her throat. It drank the deepest of her blood. A half-

The Even

opened bud nuzzled its petals against her cheek, its hue brightening as it drank.

Blood and pain. They were the most valued coin traded in the city's markets. There were few who'd turn them down.

Thick, knotted roots pushed up from beneath the earth, cracking the paving stones and pushing them aside. Clots of dark, rich earth fell from them into the fountain. The water splashed Lenith's back and hands.

"Take me down," she said. The sound of her voice made the bloom at her cheek wither. "Down amongst the dead."

The branches tightened one last time, tearing her skin, and pulled her down into the earth. It opened to welcome her and then closed over her head. The roots dragged the paving stones they'd dislodged back into place, fitting them together like a jigsaw, and withdrew back into the earth.

Lenith crawled back out of the earth at the edge of the Even Square. The wards stopped her getting any closer. She pushed herself to her feet, shaking the dirt from her hair and wiping the blood off her face. Tanit's way of travelling was less chaotic.

She was not the only one in the Square. It was rarely empty, unless ordered so by the Yekum. There were always tallymen and tinkers, orators on their soapboxes and petitioners waiting their chance to get to see the Yekum. They were in disorder now.

Some fled, dragging children and spouses along with them. Feet slipped on the wet stones and those who fell were trampled underfoot, driven under the surface of the floodwaters. Others gathered around the outskirts of the square to watch. Orators stayed atop their crates, screaming themselves hoarse as they preached this was the evidence of the truth of their gospel and claimed secret knowledge of salvation. A Glaistig, her eyes wild and staring in her grey face, danced up to a tallyman on goat feet. She tossed a handful of coins onto the stall.

"On the stone," she said. "On the stone to hold."

The tallyman must have been unmanned by fear, because he accepted the bet. The Glaistig laughed and danced away, decorative beads and braids flying.

T.A. Moore

Madness hung in the air.

Lenith pushed through the crowd, using her elbows and shoulders to clear her way. It would usually have earned her a curse, perhaps even caused a scuffle as someone took offense, but no-one paid her any heed today. Those not intent on finding some ephemeral safety were determined to have front row seats to their own destruction.

A cruciform shadow cut across the crowd. Lenith looked up to see that the Yekumi had abandoned their plotting and debauchery for this. Six of them criss-crossed the sky over the Even but none drew close. From the scattering of scorched feathers on the crackled cobbles one had tried and been rebuked by the Yekum's wards.

Lenith squeezed between two stocky Fachans and stopped at the edge of the Square. The edge of a puddle of water lapped at her feet. It wasn't too late, not quite, but there wasn't much time left either.

Tanit stood as close to the Even as she could get. She was waist deep in the water, her bright, sodden skirts floating. Her arms were thrown out and her head was turned skywards. Her expression was transported.

A scaled, hideous and unnamed thing reared up out of the water in front of Tanit. Water streamed off its sleek, curved sides. A triple-lipped mouth peeled open in its pale underbelly, showing off rows of razored teeth. It lunged forwards, striking Tanit, and bore her down into the water. The ecstatic look never slipped from Tanit's face. Blood turned the water pink and frothy.

"Gods die!" A troll screamed the warning from his perch atop a stall's awning. He sobbed and laughed at the same time, matting his dirty fur further. "Gods die and we're all damned. Who won? Who won?"

An inchoate keening sound rose from the crowd. Men tore at their clothes and fell to their knees in the water; women clawed bloody runnels from their faces and tore hanks of hair from their heads, tossing into the water as sacrifice.

Aphar crouched over the Even ha-Shetiyah. His fingers were

The Even

driven deep into its carved sides and the muscles stood out in his arms.

They strained against the bands of stone that threaded through his flesh. He had only lifted the stone a few inches. It was enough. Water gushed out, frothing around his legs, and the wet, scaled appendages tried to claw their owners through the gap to freedom.

Some of them, as Tanit's fate made clear, had already escaped.

Lenith steeled herself and walked into the water. It was cold enough to make her bones ache. Something swam between her legs, brushing against her calves, but if it was the creature it seemed to have sated itself on godflesh. She waded across the Square, stumbling over crackled cobbles, until she reached the rune-marked boundary. Her name rose behind as people noticed her, pointing her out to those who hadn't.

"Faceless! Save us, Faceless!"

"No! No! She's the one behind this!"

Scuffles broke out between the different cliques. Cobblestones were wrenched from the ground and used to dash in heads and others were drowned in the rising waters. Over it all the Yekumi spun and watched, the monsters following the spoor of their shadows.

The touch of the runes against her skin made Lenith's bones ache and burn. She made herself take another step.

The flow of water pushed against her legs, trying to force her back. The roar of it escaping was deafening.

"Aphar," she yelled. He ignored her. Lenith tried to step forwards but she had gone as far as the runes would allow. The most she could do was hold her ground. "Nameless."

He looked up from his labour. His face was drawn and strained, grey as the stone that marked his body.

"Where's Tanit?" he said.

Lenith looked around. The volume of water had diluted the shed blood to invisibility. There was nothing left of Tanit to see.

"Dead," she said. "Only shortly before the rest of us. Don't do this, Aphar. The Yekum will come soon. You cannot stand against him and you will die for this treachery."

His lips skinned back from his teeth in something that was almost a smile. He shifted his grip on the stone and braced his legs. The stumps of his wings twitched as if he was spreading his wings.

"Again?" he asked. "How many times can he kill me?"

He strained and the stone shifted a tiny amount. A thick, grey-green tentacle, wet, pink mouths opening and closing on the underside, slid through the gap. It twisted through the murky water and broke the surface. The rose-bud mouths made a wet, imbecilic gobbling noise.

"There will be no-one left to fetch you back this time," Lenith said. "Aphar, don't do this."

"Give me one good reason why I should not." The tentacle

The Even

whipped around and wrapped itself around Aphar's forearm. The tiny mouths gaped and gnawed, chewing divots from his flesh. He groaned but otherwise ignored it. "I am a pariah, Tanit, the only one who cared for me still, is dead and there will be forgiveness for trying."

A light bloomed at the very top of the Even. It was as bright as the sun that never shone on the Even. Some called upwards for aid and others urged Aphar on, before he could be stopped. There was less time left than Lenith had thought. She leant forward as far the wards would let her.

"For a start," she said. "Death is boring. Do you think Immortality grows wearying after a millennia or two? Try a century in the Deathlands. There's no risk, there's no change, there's no consequences. You are. Day after day. Why do you think I abandoned my post there, Aphar? Why do you think that if I counted out my debts in staters the coins would reach the roof of the Palace? Because I was out of my mind from boredom."

The corner of Aphar's mouth twitched.

"I have had my fill of interesting," he said.

Lenith looked down. The water was to her chest now, plastering her shirt to her breasts. She could see the glow of the Yekum as he descended. It burned in the water. She lifted her head.

"For spite then," she said. "You were Yekumi, Aphar. You know the taste of spite on your tongue, surely?"

Aphar's head dropped, ragged, wet hair hiding his face, and he gave a humourless chuckle.

"Surely I should do this for spite's sake," he said. "Every enemy I have ever had will be vexed by this, just before they die."

"Except for Prester John," Lenith said. "This is what he wants."

Aphar looked up. The light of the descending Yekum turned his Unnamed scion to a statue of ivory and marble. Aphar looked confused.

"Prester John?" he said. "What animus have I with him? He is human and you know I have no love for them. Until today the only contact I had with him was a few courtesies exchanged for

T.A. Moore

Tanit's pleasure."

The water was still rising. It was difficult to keep her feet on the ground with the tide pushing her backwards. Lenith stumbled backwards and felt something catch at her leg. She kicked it viciously, her boot sinking into pulpy flesh, and half-paddled forwards again. The wards burned her when she bumped into them.

"I had not realized you were a fool," Lenith said. "Haven't you realized it yet, Aphar? All of this was put into motion by Prester John and his Fifth Men. And your sweet Tanit. You're the only one who could do this."

"Prester John said that the prophecy..."

"Like all prophecies it was self-fulfilled," Lenith said. "Maybe Prester John had gotten tired of waiting. But think on it, Aphar. How did you get through the wards? The Yekum's magicians used the scribes book to make sure that no-one in the city could approach the stone. No-one."

Aphar's grip on the stone slackened and it slipped back, crushing the tentacle. The rows of mouths screamed and it let go of Aphar's arm. Where the skin had been eaten away stone grew to replace it.

The Yekum was close enough now that Lenith could feel the heat on the top of her skull. Most of the crowd, still watching although they were ankle-deep in water now, turned away, covering their eyes. A few, caught in the madness that drove the Maeneds to dance with the beasts that devoured them and the Selkies to draw on their seal skins, watched weeping, until their tears turned to blood and they cried out their eyes down their cheeks.

"Because I am Dust," Aphar said. "I am Nameless. To the City I don't exist. I'm no-one."

Lenith nodded, dipping her chin in the water.

"There have been, what? Twenty? Twenty five beings whose names have been struck from the memory of the city?"

"Ten," Aphar said. "Ten only."

"So few. And their crime?"

The Even

"Treachery."

"Just like you," Lenith said. "And they were all Yekumi weren't they? It's only intimacy that craves such total vengeance. So, if you needed a nameless being to breach the wards around the Even. What would you do?"

Three long, slow breaths escaped Aphar. He closed his eyes.

"I would frame a Yekumi for treason," he said. "They did this to me?"

"I told you not to dismiss the lesser blood-lines in the city," Lenith said. "Low cunning has brought down wiser beings than you."

Aphar's face twisted. He spat into the pure flood water and let go of the stone. It slammed back down into its bed, cutting off the water like a tap. The impact shuddered violently through the city. Screams of joy and despair rose about the square, but the riot calmed not at all.

"You're right," Aphar said sourly. "Spite is the best reason in the world not to do this."

A bolt of glowing light struck the air over Aphar's head. It coruscated through the runes, picking out the name of every soul in the city, and snuffed out the wards.

"Bring them," the Yekum commanded from above. His voice chimed like tarnished silver bells. Beautiful though it was, and it was clear how he had cozened the angels into sleeping with the daughters of Adam, there was no missing the corruption that lay underneath.

He withdrew, returning to the Even Palace, and the familiar dusk of the City returned. The younger Yekumi lowered the hands they'd used to hide their faces. They hovered, wings working furiously, and glared down at Lenith and their one-time kin.

The soldiers of the Yekum moved in to calm the populace with net and club.

Aphar sprawled over the Even ha-Shetiyah. His arms and the ends of his hair dangled in the swiftly receding water. He was too exhausted to acknowledge their presence.

T.A. Moore

"I am Ithik," one of them said. He looked much like Aphar, without the striations of stone marking his skin. "Son of the Yekum's first daughter. You will come with us to answer for your crimes."

Twenty-Two

Even the near-flood had not been enough to disturb the labours of the Yekum's blind scribes. Their work etching the ivory walls had not stopped. The steady scratch and scrape of their finger bones and the rattle of their chains filled the Hall.

Aphar knelt, his face hidden in his hands. It was a posture their captors echoed. No-one looked on the Yekum's face unless he invited it. Lenith stood, her hands clasped behind her back, and bowed her head politely. A puddle of dirty water, stained with blood and polish, spread around her boots. They stood like that for long minutes, the only sound that made by the scribes.

"You may raise your eyes," the Yekum's beautiful, terrible voice said.

Lenith lifted her chin.

The Yekum slouched in the embrace of the behemoth's sculpted tooth. His long legs were stretched out before him, his fine silk robes draping lean thighs, and he had his elbow braced on the arm of the throne, his head supported by his hand. Hanks of fine, silken hair hung loose and unornamented around his narrow, fine-boned features. His colourless eyes were bruised looking and his cheeks gaunt, the marks of debauchery on an ascetic's face.

Two courtesans draped themselves gracefully over the throne and his legs. They were beautiful, poised and elegant, draped in expensive silks and jewels. Anywhere else in the City their mannered loveliness would have drawn admiring looks and adoration. In the Yekum's Hall they were merely commonplace. All of the Yekum's courtesans were lovely, none more or less so than any other. It devalued them in a strange way, making them commonplace instead of prized. They watched events unfold with long, slanted eyes and sly smiles.

The Yekum ran his index finger along the pale arch of his brow. His slightly sunken chest rose and fell in a sigh.

"Twice a traitor," he said. "And more. Although I do not know what name to give the greatest crime I can lay at your door. Even genocide does not quite cover the... scale of attempting to unleash the apocalypse and destroy the world."

The muscles in Aphar's shoulders bunched and he curled his hands into fists. His knuckles pressed, white and bony, against his skin. He looked up.

"I am no traitor," he said.

The Yekum shifted, crooking his knee. The sole of his foot was smooth and unlined, like babies' skin. He smiled, with absolutely no humour, at Aphar.

The Even

"Truly?" he said. "Well, perhaps I misremember my judgement."

"I was no traitor," Aphar insisted. He started to stand up, but a blow across the shoulders from one of his guards put him back on his knees. Despite his posture he lifted his chin and stared arrogantly at his sire. "Tanit committed the crime in Prester John's service and laid the blame on me."

"Tanit was behind this?" The Yekum blinked slowly as he considered that. "A convenient tale, since she is dead and cannot speak for herself now. And even if true, it marks you as the Judas Goat of her scheme. To be a fool is not so much better than being a traitor."

The corners of Aphar's mouth twisted bitterly. He took a deep breath, nostril's flaring.

"If I am a fool then so are you," he said boldly. The fawning courtesans froze; their eyes darted to the Yekum to try and see how he wanted them to react. One of the Yekumi guard cuffed Aphar around the ear to silence him. Aphar hunched his shoulders and glared, uncowed by the slap. "I might have been their pawn but they led you like a ringed bull to market. You followed their plan every step of the way, from poisoning to UnNaming. They would never have gotten as far as they did without your aid."

The Yekumi raised his hand to cuff Aphar again. The Yekum intervened before the blow landed.

"Enough. I will allow him to speak." He waved a pale hand elegantly through the air, vaguely indicating the hive of warrens that would have been flooded if Aphar had succeeded. "I am sure that those he nearly drowned would be glad to hear his justification that he is neither a fool nor a traitor."

Aphar pressed his lips tightly together and dropped his head. He pressed his fists into the hard, still-wet flesh of his thighs. When he didn't say anything Lenith cleared her throat.

The Yekum turned his attention to her. Being the focus of his regard was like standing under one of the human's magnifying lens. There was a palpable heat in his light.

T.A. Moore

"The death god, Faceless Lenith of the Gate. Lily of the Underworld," the Yekum recited her titles in a bored voice. He quirked a pale brow at her. "Since you are not known for involving yourself in events that do not directly interest you, I assume that you have had a role to play in this. Were you another of Tanit's fools?"

The mockery in his words riled Lenith. They were all the more annoying for being true. She controlled her temper and shrugged.

"Perhaps," she said. "But I will count her death as evening the scales there."

One of the courtesans lifted her head from the Yekum's thigh. Her mouth was a sour, pinched line.

"You did not bring about her death," she said.

Lenith spread her hands gracefully. There was still blood and dirt ground into her cuticles and palms.

"Her death is still satisfying," she said. "Besides, in a way I did cause it. I was the one who brought Aphar back from the Deathlands. Without that, none of this would have been possible."

The Yekum wound his fingers through the courtesan's hair and pulled her head back painfully, like a dog on a leash. Her face creased in pain but she didn't make a sound. He didn't even look down at her.

"And you boast of this?" he said. "That you acted against my express wishes and helped a traitor escape his punishment?"

Lenith shook her head.

"I didn't," she said. The Yekum raised his brows and gestured for her to continue with his free hand. The other still held the courtesan leashed by his hip. "I may have acted unwisely, but I did not break any decree of yours nor overturn any punishment you laid down. You sentenced a Yekumi as a traitor but you struck his name from the memory of the city. All obligations and contracts were dissolved by that act, including yours. I brought Aphar back from the Deathlands, by your own laws he is not the Yekumi who was sentenced."

"Sophistry," the Yekum said coldly.

"It's the letter of the law," Lenith said. "The Yekumi's

The Even

conviction is no more legally binding than his debts."

The Yekum shoved his courtesan away. She went sprawling over the floor, her thick, red hair brilliant against the polished bone. Strands of her hair were still wrapped around the Yekum's fingers. He leant forwards on the throne, his flat eyes boring into Lenith.

"The law in this City is my whim," he said quietly. "If I wish to sentence you and that treacher to an eternity serving as an entree in my larder, I will. The only justification that I need for that is that I want to do it. Do you understand?"

Lenith inclined her head. The red-haired courtesan crawled back to the Yekum's side. He stroked her hair absently.

"I do," she said. "But that is no revelation, Seducer. Everyone in the City lives, trades and dies by your whim."

"But you, Faceless, you have drawn yourself to my attention. Most beings in the City struggle their whole lives to remain below my interest." There was a scuffling sound in the hall. The Yekum sat straighter on the Throne and watched as two of his daughters dragged a struggling, sodden Prester John into the Hall. "Such as your friend, the Prester."

Aphar hunched down into himself. "No friend of mine," he said.

"Do you think you have won?" The Yekum asked. Prester John wrenched his arms out of the Yekumi's grip. He drew himself upright, shoulders back and chin lifted, and strode towards the throne. His imperious demeanour faltered halfway to the throne when he had to stop and shield his eyes from the light.

The Yekum watched him with an amused smile playing about his mouth.

"Well, you haven't," he said. "Your plot has been exposed, your allies are dead or in captivity and you stand before me, awaiting judgement."

A tight smile touched Prester John's averted face.

"You have won nothing, Yekum. Prophecy will not be thwarted. This City will be cleansed, with fire if not with water. Do you think this is over? Do you think Tanit cannot be replaced, beloved though she was? Even I am not irreplaceable. For centuries I have walked this City, preaching to the people and they listened. They believed and now they..."

The Yekum buffed a scrape from the surface of one of his mother-of-pearl claws. Then he picked a shred of flesh from under it.

"Will do nothing," he interrupted Prester John. "Oh, a few of your Fifth Men might continue to meet and mutter against my rule but, without your charisma and Tanit's wealth, it will fade to nothing. This is Even City, Prester, not your New Jerusalem. If your people truly wished to escape into death then there are any number of gateways to take them there. That's why I'm letting you go."

Prester John dropped his arm and stared, for the first time, directly at the Yekum. The Yekum smiled beatifically at him, recalling the angelic visage he had long ago discarded.

"Did you think I didn't know?" the Yekum said mockingly. "This is my City. I see everything: your arrival, the inception of the Fifth Man, your treasons. All of it."

Tears ran down Prester John's face. He had to look away again, scrubbing his arm over his cheeks.

"I don't believe you," he said. "If you knew, you would have stopped me. Why would you let me preach revolution in the streets and do nothing to silence my message?"

The Yekum smiled and ran the tip of his tongue over his teeth, testing the point on his fangs. When he didn't answer, Lenith spoke for him.

"Because he is the Yekum. His whim rules the city; he has everything he needs and anything he wants. He is bored, Prester John, and you amused him. Like a mouse that plots to murder the cat."

Prester John shook his head violently.

"No. No, I will not accept that," he said. "I am not one of his creatures to dance for his amusement."

The Yekum laughed.

"Oh, but you are," he said, once he got control of himself. "You

The Even

are and you do, Prester. This is not even the first time that we have spoken of this. You see, the pleasure I garner from watching you scrabble around in the slums, hawking your jewels and your reputation to raise funds for your cause, is too sweet to only savour once. Tomorrow, you will find yourself at the city gates, for what you believe to be the first time. A pickpocket will rob you or a whore grab your shaft, and you will be disgusted by our degeneracy all over again."

Prester John was still shaking his head and mumbling no, over and over again. Despite his denial there was a dawning horror in his eyes. The Yekum waved his fingers at his daughters.

"Take him to the Magi," he said.

The two, beautiful winged woman took Prester John's arms and led him from the hall. He struggled free and tried to run but they caught him easily. One held him down while the other shattered his kneecaps. Then they dragged him away. The Magi could fix his knees as easily as they destroyed his mind.

"You knew?" Aphar asked. "You knew about what he planned to do?"

"Of course. Well, the Faceless' involvement caught me unawares but otherwise, yes, I did."

Aphar got to his feet and stepped forwards, hands clenched into fists and head down like a bull. Lenith did not think even Aphar would be foolish enough to attack the Yekum. However, he had not demonstrated any measure of good sense so far. She grabbed his arm to stop him. He stopped moving forwards but didn't drop his gaze from the Yekum's bright face.

"You knew I was no treacher then. You knew, yet you still sent me down to the gnomes?"

The Yekum sneered.

"You have listened to the Faceless once today, Aphar," he said. "Do not stop your ears now. You are not of my bloodline any longer. Even if you were still Yekumi you would have no right to question me. It pleased me to let Prester John's plan play out as it would. The sacrifice of one of my less exceptional get was a small price to pay for my amusement. Now, unless you want me to send you back to the Gnome King to decorate his pillar, hold your tongue."

Lenith squeezed Aphar's arm until she felt bone under his skin. He growled under his breath but subsided. The Yekum waited until he was sure that both of them were mute. He considered them both thoughtfully.

"Both of you thwarted what you knew to be my will, legal rationalizations aside. You have to be punished."

Lenith kept her grip on Aphar's arm. She could feel his blood pulse against her palm.

"I did save the City," she said.

"It wouldn't have been in danger if it hadn't been for you," the Yekum said.

Lenith shrugged one shoulder. "Or if you had not sent Aphar to the Deathlands in the first place."

The Yekum's eyes hooded.

"Do not try and threaten me, Faceless," he said. "I do not care if everyone in this city thinks I caused the flood by pissing on them from on high. My actions do not need justification. The only reason I do not have you both thrown back to the gnomes is that you... interest me. When the flood started I actually felt invigorated. Excited, if only for a moment."

"So?" Lenith asked.

The Yekum pursed his lips and stared at her. Then he flipped his hand at them dismissively.

"Get out of my city. Don't return until I have forgotten these events and your role in them."

Aphar took a breath as if he was going to say something. Lenith kicked him in the ankle to silence him. The punishment, as punishments went in the Even, was mild.

"How long do we have?" she asked.

The Yekum grabbed a handful of his courtesan's hair and pulled her up into his lap.

"Two quarters," he said. "Be outside the gates by then, or I'll flay your skin for pages of the book."

Epilogue

T.A. Moore

Lenith looked over the wares laid out on the stall. She picked one up and felt the quality of it between her finger and thumb.

"This is all you have?" she asked. "Has there been a shortage of fresh corpses in the city?"

The old, green skinned woman behind the stall snorted indignantly.

"I will have you know I stock the finest masks in the City." She snatched the mask back from Lenith and hung it carefully on its peg. Her fingers left damp stains on the leather. "I skinned this one myself, from a sixteen year old Swedish virgin with skin as flawless as mapping linen."

"Perhaps a few hundred years ago, Peg," Lenith said. "Now I could scrape better from a mangled corpse in the paupers grave."

Peg combed the mask's flaxen tresses with her hook-nailed fingers. She curled her lip at Lenith, showing her rows of

The Even

snaggled, green teeth.

"So why don't you then," she said. "I'll sell you the shovel myself."

"I'm lazy," Lenith said. "And in a hurry. Come now, Peg, I know you have better than this. I have no time to haggle with you today. Just get out the quality goods and let me choose. Something that will last. My business outside the city is likely to take a while and my face causes comment."

"True enough," Peg said. She scratched her warty chin and leant over the stall. "I have some fresher, but they cannot be worn in the Even itself. The, ah, original owners are still meant to be in possession of them. If you ken my meaning."

Lenith nodded.

"I do," she said. "Let me see."

Peg cackled and nodded.

"You never were a squeamish one, Lenith," she said. "I'll find you something good, and I'll even do you a deal on them since I've been having trouble moving them.

Peg disappeared back into the shop. While she waited Lenith looked over the Masks that were out on display: a pale, freckled face with a beauty mark over the lip, a dark skinned man's face with tribal tattoos framing the empty eye sockets and a round-face with grey curls whose loose skin hung in folds. They looked good, but when Lenith picked them up they were stiff and brittle like old paper.

They were good enough for a masque or an emergency, but

they'd not last if she wore them more than once or twice. She needed something that she could use and that wouldn't need too much care.

Someone walked up behind her. They smelt of roses and hot stone. She didn't need to turn around to know who it was.

"Where are we going," Aphar asked.

"We?" Lenith didn't bother to look around at her.

"You are the one who pointed it out, Faceless," Aphar said. "I have no-one else. My kin shun me, my lover is dead and the only person in the city who wanted me probably barely remembers his own name now."

"I see your predicament," Lenith said. "But why should I care?"

"Who else do you have?" he asked.

Peg came out of the shop with a selection of masks hanging flaccidly over her arm. She saw Aphar and scowled.

"You didn't say you needed a male face."

She laid the masks out in front of Lenith. The difference in quality between them and the first masks Lenith had looked at was obvious.

"No. I didn't did I?" Lenith picked up a mask. It had brown hair, pock-marked olive skin and heavy, sensuous features. She put it back down and checked through the rest carefully: a red-haired gamine, a middle-aged beauty and a homely one with a broken nose. None of them seemed quite right. She needed a face that wouldn't cause any sort of comment, positive or negative.

Peg watched Lenith, impatient.

"Well?" she asked. "Do you want a mask for him?"

Lenith picked up a freckled, snub-nosed mask. The original owner had pierced the nose with a small diamond. She lifted the mask up to her face and contemplated the scrawny, ancient saleswoman through the eyeholes.

"I suppose I do," she said. "Something of the same quality as mine, and unremarkable."

Peg grunted and pulled up her skirts, showing bony, vein-wrapped legs. She stomped back into the shop. Lenith turned and

The Even

showed Aphar the mask.

"What do you think?" she asked. "Will it do?"

He stared at the blonde mask and shrugged.

"Pass for what and where?" he asked

"Human and on earth," Lenith said. The revelation made Aphar curl his lip in distaste. She shrugged. "It is the best place to wait out the Yekum's irritation. You don't have to come."

He looked stubborn and crossed his arms.

"I will come," he said. "Why should I suffer alone when the fact I live at all is your fault?"

Peg came back with a few more masks that she laid out carefully on the stall. She started her sales patter but Lenith interrupted her.

"I'll take this one." She held the mask up. "Put it on the Yekum's tab."

Peg hesitated and licked her thin, wrinkled lips. Her eyes flicked towards the Palace and back to Lenith.

"You have permission?" she asked.

Lenith nodded.

"I do," she said.

It was not a claim that anyone would make falsely. The Yekum was right that most beings struggled to avoid his attention. None tried to irritate him. But Lenith would be gone by the time Peg's bill got to the Even. It would add a few more months to her exile but it was hardly a significant amount.

"Both of them," Aphar said. He had chosen the best-looking of the faces Peg had supplied. It was unsurprising considering his bloodline, Lenith supposed.

They finished their business with Peg, who could not wait to be rid of them, and headed towards the Gate out of the city. After a couple of strides Lenith cocked her head to the side.

"Prester John should be arriving at the Gate by now," she said. "The Yekum wanted him to hate the City. Let us give him a good reason for it."

It was small enough revenge, the man had played her for a fool, but it would do until she could arrange something worse. Lenith knew the taste of spite as well as Aphar.

"And then?" Aphar asked. "What will we do on Earth?"

Lenith shrugged. "What we always did, our kind," she said. "Whatever we want."

A Preview of Shadows Bloom:

Novel of The Even

Prologue

It had not been Blodeuedd's idea to become the unofficial patron of the neighbourhood around the small house she called home. Had anyone asked her, she would have declined. Never having been child or mother herself, she felt she had no particular calling to the role of guardian. Besides, she had a despite for the sort of duties and responsibilities that would place restrictions, of any sort, on her free will.

She found it galling enough to wear Lilith's mark on her hands, and the Mother-of-Demons had made little enough claim on her loyalty.

However, no one asked her. The children just found their way to her garden over the years. Just one at first, a snotty-nosed girl-child with dull eyes and skin that was more bruises than not. The girl asked for little and Blodeuedd was not heartless. It seemed harmless enough to let her hide amongst the brambles when her drunken father raged, or to let her quiet her grumbling belly on berries. One day the girl brought her little brother to the garden. Then a friend. And another.

T. A. Moore

Blodeuedd tolerated them as long as they caused no damage to her flowers and ignored them for the most part. Oh, the pimps and procurers who came sniffing around were given short shrift when they peered through the willow lattices of her fence. Blodeuedd had little time for their kind, who lived by enslaving others.

Eventually those children grew to adulthood - or died before they reached it - and Blodeuedd was left alone again. Until the first girl came back to the garden. A woman now, but still dull-eyed and with broken bones were once she'd sported bruises. Her husband came to take her back. Blodeuedd would have let him, it was none of her business, but the man tore up her plants and threatened her. He handled her. That could not be borne.

His remains served to nourish the plants he'd tried to kill.

Somehow, it set a trend.

Parents left their children in Blodeuedd's garden to grow up safe amongst the roses and lavender. They came to beg her aid when the Tallymen sent the kneebreakers round or the dealers in souls came creeping around their windows.

A Preview of Shadows Bloom

In return for Blodeuedd's aid they gave her small pouches of seeds, damp-wrapped clippings and freshly unearthed bulbs for her garden. Once her plants filled the confines of the garden and spilled out they gave her pots by their doors and window-sills to nurture things in.

To Blodeuedd, sown rather than born and magicked to life from drifts of petal, the profusion of green and growing things made Even City, where all that grew were streets and buildings, seem more like a home.

The various troubles that her neighbours sought her aid with were well within her capabilities. She possessed no great power herself, but she had been crafted and cursed by the greatest of mages. The dregs of the city that found their way to her door were little challenge.

It was a tolerable enough arrangement.

In Even City, such things could never last.

About The Author

T.A. Moore is a Northern Irish writer with a number of complicated plans to take over the world, mostly involving asparagus and a small bus. Unfortunately her busy schedule means that she probably won't be putting any of them into action before 2012 at the earliest.

A lot of people react to her work by staring at her and going, "But you seem so nice."

She takes this as a compliment. Her claim to fame is that she once drank seven shots of espresso in one go and didn't die or go into orbit. In addition to her writing career she is a tutor, a website designer, magazine editor, student and book reviewer. You can see why she needs the coffee.

Her website and plans for world domination can be found at: : www.nevertobetold.com

If only she can find enough asparagus.